TO: A

M000074869

Dragonfly

Girl

Listen to your own
Dragonfly within.

Logan Lansing

Logan

Dragonfly Girl
Copyright 2021 by W. Loos

ISBN: 978-1-7365979-2-7

Published by
Can't Put It Down Books
An imprint of
Open Door Publications
4182 Olde Judd Dr.
Willow Spring, NC 27592

Cover design by Eric Labacz, labaczdesign.com

To the courageous women of resilient spirit who have come before me, particularly the writer Erica Jong whose book, Fear of Flying, *redefined sexual equality and turned us on to the zipless fuck.*
And to all the men in my life, past and present, and the ones I've yet to meet.

Chapter One ✦

"FUCK YOU, FRANK!"

"Nice, real nice. So what are you gonna do? Run away to your muuhh-ther's?" He stretched out the word, as if the slower he said it, the more it would sting. "And come crawlin' home in three days beggin' to suck my cock?" A damp t-shirt hiked over his belly, Frank let out a deep belch as he staggered out of the 5' x 5' jail cell we called a bedroom and took two steps forward.

I backed up. "Not this time. This time I'm gone for good! I left a letter on the kitchen table. Read it. I'm filing for divorce and taking back my maiden name. Get a lawyer. I have one."

Hot August in South Jersey but no pastels for me. Today I needed a power outfit to stick to my guns: black racer back tank, black short skirt and low-heeled, laced-up black leather sandals. I glanced at the cracked, full-length mirror leaning against the chipped paint on the living room wall.

Not bad for almost thirty!

"So Su...zannne, how you gonna make money? Sellin' stale doughnuts and lottery tickets to truckers at rest stops, same as now? That's not gonna buy you a divorce." Cracking himself up as he slurred his words,

1

spit flew everywhere.

"Maybe, or I'll round up shopping carts at Walmart. For extra I could do blowjobs in the parking lot. And I'm starting with all your friends. Look, I'm linin' 'em up right now." I punched in numbers and held my phone to his face.

"Hah! Your puny licks would be worth, let's say, a dollar-fifty on the high side."

"Puny licks? How would you know?" I said, ducking his airborne saliva. "You were always dead drunk."

Grunting, Frank lurched toward me, forehead veins popping and arms flailing. It was now or never. I grabbed my previously packed bags, banged open the screen door and bolted. His voice rose as he yelled after me.

"Better count on something more than your pitiful, dry lips on pricks. Hey, Suz, wait a sec. What friends were you callin'? Fuck. Better not be Gary or Ray. And if it was Duce, I'll kill ya…"

His words trailed off as I flipped him the bird and gunned the motor of my '67 VW bus. But between the bucking, loud backfiring and swirling dust, the memorable exit I wanted to make wasn't happening. A quick glance in my side-view mirror caught the sight of my all too familiar shit-faced husband stumbling, tripping and cursing. I hoped it was the last I saw and heard of that dickhead, Frank Wilson.

BEFORE GETTING ON THE GARDEN STATE Parkway, I took the scenic route along the ocean to clear my head and inhale the briny odor of salty sea air. The familiar distant cries of children's squeals, the cawing of gulls and the peaceful repetition and rhythm of waves drew me in. As I relaxed and loosened my white-knuckled grip on the steering wheel, I caught a glint of the thin gold band around the finger on my left hand—the same gold band that had been waiting seven years for the promised matching wedding ring. Jamming the gearshift into park, I jumped out, sprinted over the sand and yanked off the ring, flinging it far into the ocean—at the same time thinking I should've sold it for cash.

Yeah, that would've been the smart thing to do.

LOUD ROCK MUSIC THUMPED FROM my car radio as I pulled into the middle lane heading north to Mom's on the Parkway. Tears built up as I cranked open the window, blew out a deep breath and sucked in freedom.

But now what?

I could spend the entire trip up to Summit, New Jersey, hoping to shake the picture of Frank's beer bloated face and trying to remember why it took seven years of marriage to leave such a loser.

Or...

I could review all the things I did before I left. Laundry washed. Garbage out. Food in fridge. Check. Check. Check. No leftover guilt, no remaining regrets. Nothing. Only anger. At myself.

But I didn't want to think about any of it, not the dilapidated trailer we lived in until the house Frank promised to build was started or the dog who lovingly stayed by my side during the whole shit-show or the education I never finished. Not about our marriage that fell apart even before the honeymoon or all the nights of Frank's lousy drunken sex moves until he passed out and I was left hanging and alone.

Or...

I could make a plan, a serious plan for my future. After all, I had two years of community college. A good start. And Mom would be thrilled to know I'd dumped Frank and wanted to go back to school. She might even pitch in some bucks. But did I want to listen to "I told you so" a million times and her ongoing insistence that I attend Al-Anon because it had saved *her* life?

The traffic picked up; I was in unfamiliar territory. Exit signs in the 130s whizzed by for Linden and Rahway. Wait! Didn't I read in the class newsletter that Jerry Spinella was now managing his uncle's bar somewhere around here? Oh, man, Jerry, my boyfriend from Summit High School before I met that lowlife Frank on the beach at the shore and threw away my future. What *was* the name of that bar? An odd name. Oh, right, Dr. Unk's. It spelled d-r-u-n-k-s. Guess that said it all.

One drink. I'll stop off for one drink and do what I should have done years ago.

The directions on my phone led me to a brick storefront building sandwiched between two tall factories, the location basically hidden and ugly. There were only two trees on the entire sidewalk, each shading the front windows of one of the factories. With all the vacant parking spaces on the street, I slid into one, adjusted the rear-view mirror in my direction and swiped on some lipstick.

Stepping down from the van, I stretched, squinted into the sunlight for a moment and shoved open the humidity-swollen door that said Dr. Unk's in scratched-up black lettering. As I adjusted my eyes to the dim entrance, I put my oversized sunglasses on top of my head, pushed back my hair and blinked my way further inside. The room was wider than it looked from the outside, with a huge bar that ran the length of the place. Tables for two or four lined the edges of what seemed like a deserted dump.

My eyes narrowed as a door swung open and a backlit body of a tall man came out from the far end.

"Jerry?" My voice echoed off the dingy walls.

"We're closed. Who wants to know?"

"It's me, Suzanne Quinlan."

The figure paused. "Suzy Q? Best ass in the class?"

I laughed. "The one and only."

I stepped closer. Wearing jeans and no shirt, he didn't move. Was he still angry after all these years?

Screw it.

I ran toward him and folded into his broad, sweaty chest. As he pulled me in, a scent memory sliced through: Jerry, me, back seat of his truck. It was after he had worked out. I loved being with him then. No fake spicy men's cologne. Just Jerry.

"Hey." I leaned back and looked up into his clear steel blue eyes ringed with dark lashes. "Even after all this time you smell like yourself."

"That's the way you liked it. Manly, you said."

And there it was. His wide grin framed by dimples, spreading sunshine through the windowless room.

How could I have given him up for Frank?

Jerry put me at arm's length, taking me all in before giving me a quick little spin. His eyes hesitated at chest level, then rested on my face. "Lookin' good, Suzanne. But come on, there's no way you were just passing through this neighborhood. Let's sit down and catch up."

As he draped his arm around my shoulder and steered me toward one of the tables, his hand slipped down and brushed my butt. I sat while he brought over two bottles of water from the bar and tried to ignore the low-level volt that hadn't left.

I licked my parched lips, gulped some water and opened up. "I made a *BIG* mistake marrying Frank Wilson. You knew it, my mother knew it, all my girlfriends knew it. But not me. I was blinded by his beach body muscles, and the fact that he had an auto body shop at the shore. He seemed like an uncomplicated, undemanding, fun guy who loved cars and had a good start-up business. Looking back, I think I was desperate for a getaway from Mom's control and Dad's drinking."

I braced myself for the usual wave of sadness that followed thinking about Dad but kept going.

"Jerry, please know it had nothing to do with how I felt about you. Anyway, you were set to go to Rutgers for the next four years. Frank's proposal seemed like the easiest solution for me. I had no idea he was an alcoholic and big bull shitter. So today I left him. It was time. Way past time."

"And you're here because…"

"Because I owe you an apology."

His eyes widened.

"I'm sorry if I hurt you, Jerry. Really sorry."

"I thought we had a good thing going. So, okay, I'll admit I was upset when you left but there was no stopping you," he swallowed hard. "Moving on, Suz, what are your plans?"

"That's the problem. I'd go back home to Summit with my tail between my legs but I hate the thought of listening to my mother. My eventual dream is to have my own business but first I need to make some money. Big money. So, maybe I'll…"

"So stay here."

"Here?"

He reached across the table and squeezed my hand. His fingers strong, his touch warm.

I scanned the empty room while his grasp remained. "You've got to be kidding. I don't see any customers."

"It's Sunday. We're closed. But during the week and Saturdays, it's jammed."

"Seriously? What's the draw? This place is dark and, uh, seedy. Don't like to hurt your feelings but just sayin'."

"Watch." Jerry slid his hands away from mine, then walked over to the sidewall with that solid, athletic stride of his and flipped several switches.

Whoa! A disco sound system kicked on in sync with revolving white and colored lights that flooded the entire bar. All the scuffed furniture and graffiti faded away. The rundown place took on a newer, almost high-end, look.

"Ohmygod, Jerry, It's beautiful. I'm impressed."

"When my uncle died, family asked me if I would

7

help save the place from going under. I agreed because they didn't want to let the liquor license lapse. I thought it would be short term but after I put in the lights and built a DJ booth," he pointed to a small stage on the side wall, "and hired some girls who could dance, the rest is history. My aim is to turn this from a bar for tired factory workers into an upscale gentleman's club for all men."

"I'm interested but what would I do? I've never bartended, and I sure as hell never stripped or danced around a pole."

"You're pretty." He leaned forward and smiled as I imagined seeing wheels turn behind his eyes. "That's a big plus. So what are your other talents?"

"Organizing and managing people. So far in my life I've sold myself short and played small. Now I want to change. And as you remember," I said in a joking, well, okay, flirty way, "I do a fairly decent blow job."

Did I just say blow job?

"Couldn't forget that, Suz." Jerry's grin grew as the memory sunk in. "Here's the deal," he cleared his throat. "What you're willing to do is going to determine how much money you'll make. Talk to my manager, Julia. She'll fill you in." He hesitated. "But I have a few ideas of my own. And I sure as hell could use a blonde around here."

Chapter Two ⊁

A BIG-CHESTED WOMAN, she was tall, maybe six feet. Despite her almost wrinkle-free face, her graying hair restrained in a tight bun made her look stern and older than her sixty-something years. When Jerry introduced us she surrounded me with a giant bear hug; any tighter and I would have lost consciousness. But she had large, brown, spirit-filled eyes and a smile that drew me in and kept me there. Couldn't help it, I liked Julia from the get-go.

Was I wrong?

She had worked at Dr. Unk's for over twenty-five years. First, as a cigarette girl and bouncer when it was a beer and shot type place, then manager for Jerry's uncle, and now for Jerry. No prude, Julia changed her attitude with the times. She was fiercely loyal; her face glowed with pride when she talked about the new look of the bar and especially the talents of the dancers. Whether stripping, working the pole or lap dancing, "my girls," as Julia called them, felt her presence and felt safe. "No funny stuff in the main room," she'd say. "Take the rest to the private rooms upstairs."

"What do you consider 'funny stuff?'" My curiosity piqued.

Her serious tone took over. "Fucking or sucking

dick on or anywhere near the bar. Everything else is a go."

"What if you didn't know it happened?"

"It better be quick," Julia came back with a deep laugh, "because I see everything. My gut sense always knows when something is up." Her laughter morphed into a girlish giggle. "But in here we hope that everybody *is* up—in one way or another." More giggling. "Please don't take offense to anything I say of a sexual nature. Booze is our business. But sex sells the booze."

"That makes perfect sense." My eyes squared on hers so she knew I was listening.

"Jerry tells me you need a job."

I opened my mouth for further discussion, but she jumped in first. "We get a big lunch crowd and need a waitress. Salary and tips okay?"

Oh man, a job. Jerry saved me!

Again, I couldn't say another word before she spoke up. "Jerry had a great idea and I agreed. We are going to have you wear a French maid's outfit—you know, short black, low-cut dress with a little white lace apron and headpiece, looking sexy. It'll give this place some class. You'll get lots of tips. Interested?"

"Very, I—" She cut me off before I could ask questions.

"Good. Can you stick around until morning? The seamstress will measure you at ten."

"I'll make sure to be here." Seamstress? For a strip bar? This place is nuts. Nuts! Julia, who connected every word to sex, would probably say in here our customers usually have two.

"If you need a place to sleep tonight, we have

10

blow-up mattresses in the girl's dressing room."

"No thanks, I'll camp out in my van."

Julia made a face. "Doesn't sound very comfortable."

"It's a restored VW bus, and it's more comfortable than the trailer I lived in for the past seven years."

"Suit yourself. See you tomorrow." She moved toward the door but turned back and waved. "Glad you're with us, Suzanne."

As Julia walked away I could see some tendrils had loosened themselves from her taut upswept hairstyle. The delicate swirls surrounding her face gave her a softer, younger look. Maybe I'd tell her that in the morning. Or not. Probably overstepping.

I drove my van into the bar's rear parking lot. Scrubby bushes lined the back property that separated the bar from another street of large factories. Low-hanging trees shaded a small area in one corner. The remains of scattered litter made me think it was a spot used for the dumpsters that were now wedged closer to the bar's back kitchen door. I pulled in and parked. A perfect fit for my VW bus. And for privacy.

IT TURNED OUT THE SEAMSTRESS, Bella, was the mother of Isa, one of the dancers. Why a mother would want her daughter's career choice to be a go-go dancer in a strip bar was beyond me but I wasn't going there.

Abracadabra! After the measuring, the sewing was finished in one day. Bella, Isa and Julia nodded their approval of my new skimpy outfit and led me to a full-length mirror.

"Wow! Look at me, a real live bar room Barbie."

My whirling and twirling was cut short as I caught Jerry's reflection in the mirror.

"One word," he said, flashing me a megawatt smile. "Bombshell!"

I turned and threw my arms around his neck, weaving one hand up and through his thick and tousled chestnut-brown hair. Without warning he pushed back and unwound himself. His actions landing like a gut punch. Isa and Bella fled the room. Jerry followed.

Julia grabbed my arm. "Listen, Suzanne, that had nothing to do with you. Isa's been sleeping with Jerry, and hearing his reaction to you brought out some jealousy."

I sucked in. "Does he sleep with *all* the dancers?"

"This is no Sunday school, and Jerry's no choir boy," she clipped her words. "A little advice. I know you used to date Jerry but stay out of his business now. He tends to hump and dump. I've never seen him be serious. And you know men: nothing like new pussy."

So that settled that. Hands off Jerry. Served me right. I sold him out for that shithead Frank years ago. In a way his brush-off was a gift. Gave me more time to concentrate on making money.

But still…

Chapter Three ⊁

AFTER THREE WEEKS OF WAITRESSING in fishnet stockings and high heels, my feet and back ached and the corners of my mouth hurt from continually smiling. Total sum of salary and tips saved: a few hundred dollars. A math major in high school and not stupid, I knew that amount wouldn't get me an apartment any time soon. Further evidence I was a loser. There must be something else I could do to make more money. After all, Jerry said my willingness would determine how much I could make.

In downtime between serving lunch and dinner, I watched how Julia not only acted as a bouncer, taking no shit from the aggressive and disorderly types, but also managed the girls, ordered the food and booze and took care of all the paperwork. It was a job I felt I could handle. But it was taken.

The dancers and strippers made more than their salary from tips shoved down their G-strings while gyrating on the bar or pole, from doing lap dances, and of course those upstairs rooms where they did all kinds of who knows what else.

That's it. Time I asked Jerry what other jobs were available. But secretly, I wanted to talk to him, look at him, be close to him. The problem was he only came

13

out of the kitchen or DJ booth for a short time after food was served to say hello to the lunch and dinner customers. I checked the clock behind the bar. Five minutes to go.

"Jerry, wait. Can I speak to you?" I used my sexiest voice, made sure my hair was casually perfect and reapplied my lipstick carefully, playing up the Cupid's bow in my top lip. Jerry always loved my full, pouty, kissable lips.

"What's up, Suz? I'm busy," he said with his back to me, clearing last night's dishes from the tables.

"Jerry, please, I need to make more money. What else can I do?"

"Guess you could be a bottle girl," he said as he took off toward the kitchen, never even glancing my way. "Can't talk now. Too busy. See Julia."

That stung! He sure as hell hadn't been too busy to put his dick in my mouth in that beat-up truck of his in the high school parking lot. Now he couldn't even talk to me?

Julia, Jerry's self-appointed bodyguard, hurried over. Man, that woman didn't miss a trick.

"What's going on, Suzanne? Didn't I tell you not to bother Jerry?"

"He told me I could make extra money as a bottle girl—and to talk to you."

"Okay, but ask me first next time, not Jerry. We have a no-nonsense policy here."

No-nonsense policy? What the hell was that?

"I give up, Julia," I said, changing the subject, "what's a bottle girl?"

"Come to the bar and I'll get you set up."

I dutifully followed her, feeling like some kid

called to the principal's office. After Julia asked the bartender if there were any requests for a bottle, I assumed I would be delivering it to someone's table.

But no.

"We call what's upstairs the exclusive VIP Floor. There are private dining rooms and champagne rooms where lap dances are, let's say, expanded, and there are several exclusive bedrooms for overnight guests and their activities. Tonight the gentlemen in room three want a very expensive wine and some glasses. You must arrange everything on one of those silver trays found underneath the bar. Add a few fancy napkins and a handful of candy mints."

I watched her face for approval as I followed her directions but her expression remained flat and firm.

"Now go upstairs, knock once quietly and wait. Don't barge in. Even a small distraction might jeopardize how much money our girl in the room makes. Got it?" I nodded. "It's not Candy Land on the second floor so remain calm, and don't get flustered with anything you see. Remember, we're not selling Girl Scout cookies up there."

Carrying a tray with a bottle and fancy cut glass goblets up a flight of stairs in high heels was a recipe for disaster. But I made it. I stood for a second, taking in the guest room hallway. Like a ritzy old hotel it had high ceilings, tall gold-framed mirrors, dusty blue satin striped wallpaper and carpeting in an old-fashioned pattern of large and small pink roses. Heavy wooden doors with a brass number on each kept the sounds of those inside private. I passed room number one, then two and stopped at room three. Uh oh. The door was open a few inches. I peeked in. The lighting was low

15

due to the heavily draped floor to ceiling windows, but I could make out a bed with a naked girl on her hands and knees between a man's legs. Her long, dark hair fell down in front of her face, covering the obvious head she was giving. Not disturbing her rapid up and down movements, the man reached out and yanked up her hair to see the action.

Oh my God, it's Isa! Does Jerry know what she's doing?

Of course he knows. She's just a piece of meat to him like I was in the high school parking lot.

Should I knock? Or leave and return when they're done? As I turned to go, another naked man walked toward the bed from the bathroom.

Oh, man, she's doing two guys!

"This one's for you, sweetheart," Man Number Two said as he crawled onto the bed. Positioning himself behind her upturned ass, he entered her cunt with one punishing shove of his monster dick and began pounding. His balls slammed up against the back of her thighs in a loud rhythmic drumbeat. "How do you like that, baby?"

With Man Number One's shaft in her mouth, Isa gave out a muffled scream, then grunted with each determined push. I'd seen some porn flicks with Frank but this was different. This was real.

Real ugly.

But I was transfixed—and aroused. A wave of heat shot through my body. With one hand, I wedged the tray into the side of my waist as my other hand drifted down under my short French maid skirt and inside my black lace panties. As my two fingers circled and stroked my throbbing clit, I watched the guy's in

16

and out thrusts.

Oh, oh yeah, oh yeah. Faster, faster. Uh, uh, ah, ah, ahhh... I'm coming...

While trying to regain my balance, I fell sideways into the room. The whole tray—expensive wine, glasses and all—hit the floor with a gigantic *CRASH!*

Man Number One getting the blowjob and Isa stopped and stared. Man Number Two got the picture and pulled his huge dick out of her and walked toward me. "Hey, you're going to pay for this wine," he snarled, "unless—"

"Unless what?" Cold sweat slid down my back.

"Start by sucking my cock," he said, stroking his erect sledgehammer, pushing it into my face, "and then you can see how her pussy tastes."

Grossed out, I drew back. "I'm just the bottle girl. I, I'll get fired."

"Okay then," he hoisted me up from a fallen heap, "stand by me and look pretty while I finish fucking Jerry's bitch. Maybe you'll learn something."

I exhaled sharply. "I, I can do that."

As Man Number One pulled Isa's head down and jammed his dick back into her mouth, she shot me a sideward glance. Our eyes locked. Tears were pooling up and sliding down her beautiful face, landing silently onto the rumpled blue satin sheets.

Man Number Two got back on the bed, spanking each of Isa's ass cheeks again and again with his big cock. She whimpered and squirmed as he dug into the flesh on either side of her butt like handles, pulling her toward him and slamming himself into the slit between her legs. And until he came and slumped over her back, his eyes never left my face. Not once.

17

Chapter Four ✈

I COULDN'T SHAKE IT; THAT GROSS memory loop played day and night in my brain. Poor Isa. Sexually jack-hammered from behind. I was jealous of her with Jerry but, after seeing what she did, what she *had* to do for money, forget it. How much did she make? Not frigging enough. Clearly, that was rape for cash.

Is this how it always had to be? Women giving, men taking. The way I saw it a woman's used-up body and worn-out self-esteem were the collateral damage after men got theirs. But then again, money was to be made here at Dr. Unks. Maybe something not so extreme and certainly less harsh.

Slow down and don't rush into anything, I told myself. Ouch, it sounded familiar. "Poor impulse control and prone to risk taking"—those were the words one of my teachers used on my senior year report card. "Suzanne has so much potential but seems lost," another teacher remarked. When I first read those comments, I thought, *What the fuck do they know?* Now I saw they knew a lot. And apparently, I had much to learn from failures, starting with my dumpster fire of a marriage. I looked down. My fists were clenching, and I felt my jaw tighten as I remembered how I followed my own Yellow Brick

Road into Hell. Now, hopefully, I was finding my way back. While keeping my teacher's words in mind, making a few bucks doing "a little social service" might speed up the process.

Perhaps? Nah, Jerry would never approve. But what if he didn't know? Should I talk to Julia tomorrow? She said she knew everything that went on inside Dr. Unk's but what about outside? Wasn't my van my own territory?

BJs in the parking lot. That's it!

To tell Julia or not to tell Julia? That was the question. And would she rat me out to Jerry? But so what? Jerry and I were history. My desperation for money overrode everything but I knew that doing anything behind Julia's back would get me fired—and fast. First thing tomorrow morning I would tell her my plan and ask for her help. As they say, I needed to put money where my mouth is.

In bed that night my mind automatically wandered back to room three. To erase that sickening and cruel memory, I quickly switched to thoughts of Jerry and how I remembered his beautiful stiff dick. My fingers teased my already pulsating clit as I thought about practicing on him.

I knelt over him. His hips lifted but I reached up and pressed my hand on his chest.

"Lie back," I whispered, "relax."

Little by little my mouth slid lower and lower, taking my time before I engulfed the rest of him in one last accelerated downward dive. Pulling up, I held his giant erection tightly between my hands and lips. I moved rhythmically up and down, increasing in urgency until he cried out, shuddering repeatedly with each hot surge and my immediate draining swallow. Finger-licking delicious!

I finished myself off with my ever-ready vibrator but wished there were someplace I could go, like men, to get a happy ending. Being female was definitely a DIY project, especially when you were married to someone like Frank. Clearly, his serious alcohol problem had put the brakes on my blowjob skills and, hell, just plain screwing over the years. I tried, but a drunk's limp dick stays that way. But what about me? What about girls like Isa? Nobody ever took time with us. Something was wrong. I turned over and let sleep wash away my thoughts of years of unfulfilled and unsatisfactory sex. Money was now my priority. Tomorrow would be a good day. Julia would like my plan. I was certain.

"Do you know what you're doing with these?" Julia said the next morning, snatching and holding up my hands in front of me.

"Huh?" I replied still stunned she had given her approval to my idea of doing BJs in the parking lot.

"A blow job, a hand job or a combination of both is *not* just up and down, then you're done. Every man is different, every dick is different, the time he needs is different, his preferred position is different—"

"Okay, okay. I get it. All different. Sounds like you know a lot. Could you teach me? Please?"

"I don't have much time, but I'll try. When do you want to start?"

"Now."

"So much to learn, so much to teach." Julia sighed

and checked the clock behind the bar. "It's nine now. We'll have a lesson until ten. Customers will be coming in then. You'll have to put on your outfit for lunch, and I'll have to check the bar and food inventory."

"Thank you, Julia. But what the hell is going to take an hour?"

"An hour is just the start. You'll see." She chuckled and disappeared into the kitchen.

Returning after a few minutes, Julia carried two cucumbers, a handful of condoms and some latex gloves. What's so difficult? She'd put the rubbers on the veggies and we'd be good to go.

"Do you know how to put a condom on a man's dick without using your hands?"

"Wouldn't they put it on themselves?"

"Time is money," she said, handing me a cucumber and rubber. "You're in business now. This isn't high school fun times in the back seat. With a condom on you don't ever have to worry about spitting or swallowing. And you want it on fast, and never, never, NEVER do you want to participate in unprotected fellatio!"

"Fellatio. That's a blowjob. Right?"

Julia rolled her eyes and mumbled something about seeing the need to start from scratch.

Instructing me to follow her lead, she sucked the condom tip into her mouth. I thought it looked ridiculous with the roll of the rubber around the outside of her lips but Julia assured me most men find anything you're going do with their cocks very hot. As she drew the condom further into her mouth, she gripped the cuke at the base and let her lips slide

21

slowly down the veggie and unroll the condom. Man, she made it look so easy. After four awkward tries I imagined it was Jerry's prick. That's when I got the idea and slid it on to her satisfaction.

"Woo hoo!" I hoisted my latex covered cucumber high. "Who said it's not easy being green?"

"Now," Julia announced, completely ignoring my attempt at humor. "We've got twenty minutes to discuss gloves."

"Gloves?" I lost it. "Why? Is this a formal occasion?" I was laughing so hard I almost missed her tight mouth and threatening glare.

"Suzanne, do you want to make money or not?"

"Sorry, Julia. Yes, desperately. That's my goal."

"Okay, moving on. Are you allergic to latex?"

I shook my head, no.

"Good. Latex gloves can be helpful if you incorporate your hands into oral sex. It's a safe sex practice and protects you from picking up any STDs."

"But gloves are so, so clinical. Don't men want the feeling of skin on skin?"

"Trust me. If you know what you're doing and do it well, they will enjoy all the sensations you create but it's up to you if you want to use them. Oh, dear, our time's up for now. Would you like to continue after lunch, say between three and four?"

"Yes. Thank you, Julia. Why don't you come to my van for the afternoon session?" I said as I gathered up the cucumbers, condoms and gloves. After my morning "learning opportunity," as Julia called it, I wanted to take a nap, but I had to serve lunch in my French maid's outfit. Perhaps I could keep my eyes open for some possible customers.

Customers!

The word made me shudder. Jeff, Cliff, Donnie and sweet Jimmy, okay. Lonely losers like Dooley, Nick and a guy named Iggy? No way. But how do you not do the ones you don't want to do? Julia would have the answer. Just thinking about Cliff, however, gave me a little clit tingle.

Chapter Five ⸕

Right on time Julia knocked at my van door with a box tucked under her arm. "Hey, this isn't as bad as I thought," she said, looking around. "Actually, it's kind of cozy. Now let's teach you to suck some cock."

"One question first," I said as she unpacked the box. "What if I don't want to do, let's say, Iggy? He's so creepy and hardly sexy, a real turn-off."

"Once again, Suzanne," Julia eyeballed me, "do you want to make money or not? All the girls here take care of everyone who goes upstairs with them. You can't be choosy. And word has it Iggy's cock is very nice and very large."

I didn't care how large he was. I needed a way to sort out guys I didn't want to do.

"Now pay attention." Julia could see I was distracted. "This," she said, holding up a large tube, "is your best friend."

"Oh, I know what that is. Lube. I don't need it. I use my own saliva."

"Yes, we were all born with lots of saliva but after you do one or two Iggy-type big dicks, you will run dry. And besides, lube gives both you and your customer a wonderful feeling of sliding and gliding, not stopping and starting from hitting dry spots." She paused. "Somehow," her eyes narrowed down, "I don't think you've processed the fact that you are now a sex worker."

Sex worker! That hit home.

"No, I will be doing blow jobs, only. Nothing like the girls upstairs. That doesn't make me a prostitute or whore, does it?"

"If it walks like a duck and quacks like a duck—"

"Times have changed, Julia. These days even some teenage girls give head on the school bus."

"Do they get paid?"

"Well, no. Taking money, Suzanne. That's the difference."

"Shit." My throat tightened around the word. "Guess I'm about to cross that line."

"I understand your need to survive, and making fast money is part of that. But when you get on your feet, what you've done will all be in the past. It will be your little secret."

*My **dirty** little secret.*

"Now let's talk about my favorite subject: penises."

That got my attention.

"Sexual anatomy is tricky for a male. They're proud to have that appendage, and you must never say anything they might find shaming. No matter if they have a python in their pants or they're hung like a hamster, tell each one their dick is perfect—if the subject comes up." Waves of Julia's laughter. "Up. Get it?"

"Got it. Please continue. I need this information."

"There are several types of men you need to know

about. One is the uncircumcised. It's like hitting a speed bump as you do your blowjob. Just keep going and you'll get used to it. The next is the premature ejaculator. He may come before he gets the condom on. Don't embarrass him. He lacks control and can become very aroused just thinking about getting blown. Then there's the man with such a huge one he may have difficulty getting that big baloney up and stiff. Just suck him with or without a full erection. He'll enjoy it either way. Last, but certainly not least, is the little guy. Perhaps a grower, not a shower. Actually, the lesser endowed are often fabulous under the sheets. They tend to put extra effort into pleasing a woman to make up for their size. And while going down on them the whole enchilada fits easily into your mouth. No problem.

"And that, my dear Suzanne, is the long and short..." she added a string of girlish giggles "...of penis quirks. Uh oh, time's up."

Checking her watch as she walked toward the van door, Julia turned. "Two last tips. First, some may require extra work because they've taken a little blue or orange pill to get a strong hard-on. In that case you can charge a bit more for your time. Second, some men may want you to shove your pinky up their ass toward the end of the blowjob. It's a mini massage to the prostate and helps them come. But do ask first."

"Maybe I *will* use those gloves."

THE NEXT DAY AT LUNCH I whispered to Cliff about what I was doing in my van. I thought we had some sexual chemistry; every lunchtime he'd put a ten-dollar bill down my dress. On my break I ran out to my van and changed into my sexy black bikini. I was ready for my first customer.

Showtime!

He knocked, and I invited Cliff inside. After taking off his pants, he sat on the edge of my bed and began to play with himself. My breathing sped up, and I shivered as I put on the latex gloves and knelt on the floor between his legs.

Life sucks. And now I have to suck, too.

Getting started, I gently pushed his hands away and clasped his long but somewhat thin cock at the base. Quickly, I sucked the tip of the already opened condom into my mouth, then slowly unrolled it all the way down the length of him. As he leaned back, moaning, I tongued the sides of his shaft with long ice cream cone licks as I teased the top with my fingers.

Pausing, I tasted something wet and salty. Did the condom break? I looked at my black smeared fingers. Mascara! Tears were welling up and spilling down my face, lips and into my mouth as I swayed back and forth, finally pushing away from Cliff. "I can't, I can't, I just can't." Heaving and gasping, I tried to regain control when the van door burst open. Twisting around, I saw Jerry standing in the doorway.

"What the hell is going on, Suzanne?"

"None of your business," I shot back and jumped up.

Cliff attempted to stand and cover himself but slipped and fell. He grabbed his pants, pulled out a fistful of money and reached up to shove it down my bikini top.

Hyperventilating and blubbering, I cut him off.

"No. Stop. I don't want to be a fuckin' sex worker for you or anybody else."

Lunging, Jerry made a grab for Cliff's arm and pulled him outside, slamming him up against the van. Cliff broke free, avoiding Jerry's oncoming punch, and took off. Jerry chased him, I guess to make sure he didn't come back for seconds.

Reeling and weaving, I made my way up front and collapsed into the driver's seat. Digging some tissues out of my purse, I blew my nose and mopped up my runway make-up. I could see Jerry in my rear-view mirror motioning frantically as he ran back toward my van. I slapped all four door locks down. No way could I face him after my total clusterfuck.

Now what?

I started the engine and drove out of the parking lot. After one last backward glance at Jerry, his arms hanging limply by his sides, I headed for the Garden State Parkway.

Chapter Six ⤼

I pulled off at the first rest stop. Sliding on flip-flops, I threw a red tank and jean cut-offs over my black bikini. Inside, I did a quick pee, gulped down some iced coffee and texted Mom. Said I was on my way to see her and would be there in a half hour or so. Calling would take too long with all her who, what, when and why questions. On the way back to the van, I got her return text: *I can't wait!!!* I smiled. She always did overdo the exclamation points.

I could smell fear-sweat coming from my moist pits as I rounded my tree-lined block in Summit. At worst, talking about Dad's death or Mom wringing her hands and wanting to know all about my marriage to Frank. And, oh geez, thank God she had no idea I almost became a sex worker.

Guilt. The gift that keeps on giving.

As I dragged two black plastic garbage bags full of my clothes up the well-manicured walk lined with orange day lilies and knocked on the front door, Buddy—our white Jack Russell terrier with two brown patches, one over each eye—scooted from around back and jumped into my arms. He was just a puppy when I left but, obviously, had no difficulty remembering who

29

I was. He licked my cheek, and I warmed to his affection, glad at least somebody loved me—screw-ups and all.

"Buddy beat me to it," Mom squealed as she opened the door and gathered us both up in her arms. "Come on in, sweetie, I'm so glad you're home. Hey, did you know Jerry's been calling here? At least three times in the last hour. Doesn't he know your cell phone number?"

"Sorry if he's bothering you, Mom. I've blocked his number."

"No bother but last time we talked you told me you were working for him as a waitress." Her face looked so excited, so hopeful. "So why would you block him?"

"Long story, Mom. But that job's not right for me, and neither is Jerry."

"Oh, I'm sorry. You used to like him so much. And he treated you so well. Couldn't you—"

"No, I couldn't." I knew Mom had always liked Jerry and she'd continue until she got some sort of satisfactory answers. "How about if I unpack and then I'll call him back, okay?"

"Yes, that would be the polite thing to do, Suzanne. After all, he did give you a job when you needed one."

Being polite was important to my mother. Like standing when an adult came into the room or shaking hands and saying, "How do you do?" I told her it was okay to say hi these days, but I knew as long as I lived at home she would insist on those kinds of formalities.

After I dragged my stuff upstairs to my old room, I sat on my bed and called Julia. She picked up immediately.

"Are you okay, Suzanne? Jerry's been very unhappy since you left."

"I know. He's called my mother a bunch of times. I was afraid he'd fill her in about, uh, you know, everything. And by the way, are you the one who told Jerry what I was doing in my van?" I'm sure she could sense the edge in my voice.

"To make a long story short, it seems that Cliff was so excited you were in business, he told all the lunch guys. Frankly, he thought he was being helpful. They all lined up outside the kitchen back door ready to go into your van and take their turn as soon as Cliff was finished. One glance out the window into the parking lot and Jerry knew something was going on. He quickly rushed to your defense, of course. So, no, I wasn't the one who told Jerry. And that's the truth."

"Just so you know, I couldn't go through with it. I love the idea of making fast money, but it's not for me, although I sure did learn a lot from you. Hey, I got the condom on Cliff just right. You would've been proud!"

Julia's larger-than-life laugh echoed through the phone and made me laugh, too.

"Well, there are several good sex practices we never covered. First, how to work around the gag reflex, another what to do when a guy has difficulty coming, then there's the twist, and, last but not least, the sensual magic of the optical illusion. When you're ready, just give me a call."

"Wait, Julia, you can't leave me hanging. Give me the scoop on just one. Pleeease."

"All right, just one. Picture this: What if you've done your best blow job, the guy hasn't come and

31

you're totally exhausted. What's the solution?"

"Uh, I give up. Tell me."

"The answer is call in the cavalry."

"Cavalry? As in troops?"

Julia's laugh was at roar level. "No, my dear. Get a willing friend to relieve you. It gives you a break and the guy gets even more aroused with a new girl sucking his cock."

"Ah. I get it. But where do I find this willing friend?"

"That, my sweet Suzanne, is your problem."

Before I hung up she promised to calm Jerry down and tell him I was okay, and I promised to send back the French maid's outfit. Good riddance to that thing.

It felt so good to lie back on my old bed. Mom hadn't changed anything in the room. When things got bad with Frank, I always hoped it would be exactly the same, waiting for me if I ever I came home.

Home. That word sounded really good right now.

When I woke up the sun was going down. Light from my bed lamp lit Mom going through one of my garbage bags.

"I thought I'd help and get a jump on your laundry. But I don't know what to do with this?" She held up the French maid's outfit.

"Oh, uh, that's my Halloween outfit. I, um, borrowed it but tomorrow I'll send it back to my friend Julia."

"Do you still go Trick or Treating? At your age?"

"No, Mom. I sometimes went to Halloween parties with Frank."

"Frank. Now tell me what really happened, what went wrong?"

32

I didn't want to go there but at least the subject of Frank got her off the French maid's outfit.

"Wait. Don't tell me yet. Let's go down to the kitchen. Since you called this afternoon, I've been making your favorite dinner: lasagna, salad, the whole works."

"Lasagna. Yours is the best!" I meant it as I put my arm around her shoulders and steered her out of my room. Who knows what else I stuffed into those black garbage bags?

✦

AFTER DINNER AND SHARING a small bottle of red wine, we sat on the back patio and watched Buddy trying to catch fireflies. They were too fast for him so he lay at our feet and resorted to chewing sticks. There was a chill in the night air, and I was about to suggest we go inside.

"Oh, look," Mom's voice rose in excitement, "there's a dragonfly skimming over the water in the birdbath."

The insect turned, stopped mid-air, dove, then pulled up and hovered while looking straight at me.

"It's a good omen, Suzanne," she whispered. "Supposedly, they symbolize transformation and change that produces maturity. Sort of like the dragonfly does during its own life."

I moved closer but it flew backwards for a moment and darted away.

"So beautiful, don't you think, with that blue-green iridescent body and four wings? I haven't seen one in a while." A glow spread over her face. "It must have visited here just to see you!"

I blew out a long sigh and pulled the collar of my lightweight jacket a little tighter around my neck. "Mom, I don't think I've been this relaxed in years. Love the dragonfly info and the fabulous dinner but most of all for letting me crash into your life."

"You are my only child. I've always kept the front lamppost lit for you. This house isn't just a roof over your head; it will always be your *home*. And Daddy would have wanted you here, too. Speaking of Daddy—"

"Let's not, Mom. I'm really tired."

Her face mirrored disappointment.

"Maybe tomorrow, okay?"

"Suzanne, what I want to say is about you and not about Daddy, well, not exactly. The truth is you had a father who was an alcoholic, and then you married Frank, another alcoholic. There are no coincidences. I'm sorry you were raised in that kind of turmoil. But you need to get to an Al-Anon meeting to understand yourself and your part in relationships so you don't make the same mistake again. Al-Anon has been my saving grace. And if you want to live here, I'd like you to go, too."

And there it was. Her bargaining chip.

"Okay but I don't want to go anywhere around here. You never know who might show up."

"Doesn't matter where you go, just so you go. The meetings and the friendships you make could transform your life in a positive way."

"About my life—"

It was time for a subject change.

"Got any suggestions? I'm tired of trying to convince myself I'm okay while inside feeling like a

34

loser."

"You're certainly not a loser. I recall when you were a little girl you sold lemonade, cookies and hand-painted rocks from a table out on our lawn. It was amazing how you'd wave people down and out of their cars, then coax them to buy something. Soon you graduated to making beads, bath salts and soaps, selling them at local fairs and church bazaars. Daddy and I marveled at your head for business and your growing bank account. And when you lined up other kids to sell things for you, we used to joke that you had your own sales force. That strength you had then is still inside you. You see, my dear, nothing in life is ever wasted."

"You're right. I did have loads of ingenuity and confidence. First thing tomorrow I promise I'll investigate job opportunities and school—and maybe even go to an Al-Anon meeting."

A bright smile unlocked her strained face.

"But right now I want to get into my very own bed and get some sleep."

"Perfect, sweetie. But before you begin your new life," she winked, "I'm going to give you something tomorrow to make your research flow a bit easier."

Funny, my mother never winked.

In my upstairs bedroom I opened my top dresser drawer where I kept the oversized t-shirts I used to wear to bed: Daddy's t-shirts. I put one over my head and inhaled as it fell past my hips. He'd been gone seven years but some faint Daddy smell of Old Spice aftershave and pipe smoke remained. Sitting on the bed, I hugged my knees and rocked.

Oh, Daddy, why did you have to go for a drive

after drinking at my wedding reception?

I stopped and refused to go any further down the rabbit hole of despair with visions of my father mangled in his car on the railroad tracks. I pulled off his t-shirt, shoved it back in the drawer and switched it for one of my own. After climbing into bed I yanked the sheet over my head—as if that would block out the loss of my father, the loss I hadn't been able to shake for what seemed like forever.

Drifting off into the early stages of sleep, my mind took me to a different place as I caught sight of my old bookcase in the corner alcove—the bookcase Jerry and I rescued from a garage sale, stashed in his truck and carted upstairs to my bedroom. I thought about how he just stared at me after we got it in place, one hand braced on the top shelf, his worn denim shirt drenched in sweat, and how I enticed him to take it off by saying my parents weren't home.

"Only if you take yours off, too," he shot back.

I never could resist a challenge.

Pulsating waves engulfed my clit as I fingered and played, remembering how we danced naked in the dark to our favorite slow songs on the radio and how he pulled me into his arms and lifted my chin until our lips met and his tongue slipped into the wetness of my mouth. Everything else in the room that night blurred out as I rubbed my tightened nipples against his broad chest while his growing erection pushed into me. I remembered the soft background music and Jerry's words as he nuzzled his face along my neck and whispered into my ear: "I'm crazy about you, Suzanne. I want you. Now, tonight. But first I want to explore."

As his hand moved down toward the moist

36

entrance between my legs, heat flooded my entire body. Closer, closer, his fingers inched ever closer until headlights from my parents' car turning into our driveway flashed through my window. That was the first time we almost—

Cut the fantasizing. Jerry is fucking other women. It's over.

Chapter Seven ⊁

I woke to a loud, grinding sound. Taking the stairs two at a time, I flew down to the kitchen, thinking the dishwasher was going to explode. It was only Mom tossing handfuls of green vegetables into a blender.

"Making a green smoothie," she yelled over the noise.

"Gross. What happened to pancakes?"

"My pancake days are over," she said and turned off the machine. "Eating healthy is how I'll look and feel good in my golden years. Here, try a sip." She shoved the shaker filled with green sludge toward my mouth.

Cooperation. High on Mom's mother-daughter relationship list. So I chugged.

I made a face and tried not to gag until I tasted the flavor. "Better than it looks. Guess it's a way to get in all your daily vitamins and nutrients."

"You were always such a good sport, Suzanne. Now here's another new thing to try." She took a small piece of creased paper out of her bathrobe pocket and placed it on the kitchen table in front of me. "You were really wound up last night. This will help you relax."

White on the outside, unfolded it was a day glow

iridescent blue. Not waiting for me to read the black printing, she jumped in. "It's from Massage Time over in Pleasant Hill. I bought a package of twenty sessions a few weeks ago. I'm willing to share."

"Whoa, Mom. A massage? Do I really want some strange lady's hands all over me? And probably with my clothes off?" But then I quit questioning and thanked her, remembering she called me a good sport.

"My pleasure, sweetheart. Go in and ask for Evelyn. Her Swedish massage with a light touch is the best. That's the type I always get. Please don't be upset but I called them first thing this morning and reserved a late afternoon appointment. Just make sure you park in the back. To save gas in your van, you can borrow my car and, no, Suzanne, you don't have to be naked—unless you want to be."

"Good thing." I smiled and stepped even further out of my comfort zone. "Hey, I think I'll have one of those green drinks of yours."

With the air conditioner cranked up in Mom's old green compact Ford, my phone's GPS took me about fifteen minutes on a quick drive west from Summit to Pleasant Hill. Just the town's name made the tension lift as I drove away from the chaos of the hot highway and entered the cool, shaded streets.

Scouting out the address, I easily found Massage Time. It was an odd-looking, tall, thin building nestled between large oak trees on Honeywell Drive at the end of a small strip mall. Parking in the front seemed less complicated than going around the block to the rear like Mom suggested.

Entering, I looked for a lobby. There was none, only space enough for two black folding chairs, a tiny table loaded with Hollywood gossip magazines and a wide, black wrought iron spiral staircase in the center that basically took over the whole clean and tidy room. Three walls were painted white but the fourth was papered with what looked like a blue-green design. On closer inspection I saw it was clusters of dragonflies that made it look like iridescent stained glass.

Again with the dragonflies!

"Hello, hello," I yelled.

"Up here," someone shouted back.

The black wrought iron stairs took three upward circular twists around, letting me off in front of large glass doors with chrome handles.

How the hell would anyone out of shape make it up here?

Inside, sitting at a long table facing me, was a girl with teased bleached blonde hair in desperate need of a root job and lipstick the color of a new fire engine. A three-headed dragon tattoo began at her shoulder, trailed down her arm and ended with a barbed tail at her wrist. "Coulda taken the elevator, ya know."

"Elevator? I didn't see one."

"Probably because it's down there against the wall covered with that buggy-lookin' blue paper." She cracked her gum twice and blew a small bubble. "Whatta ya here for?"

I handed her the prepaid coupon from my mother. "I was told I could have Evelyn."

"Nah. She quit yesterday. But we have this temp guy, Javier Ruiz." Her smile expanded as her pink glittered nails clickity-clacked as she typed. Turning her laptop toward me, she announced, "Here, see. This says he's been a massage guy at a lotta good places in California and New York."

Naked and alone in a room with some unfamiliar temp massage guy? No way.

"Excuse me but are you the owner?"

"Nope, I'm her cousin, Nicki-with-an-i-not-a-y. She put me in charge 'cause she's at the bank sellin' the place.

Selling? Probably due to expensive court cases brought by heart attack victims who collapsed on those circular stairs.

"I'll still be able to get a massage today, right? Oh, and are there any women working or just Javier?"

"Just Javier."

"Okay. Let's get this over with."

"You're going to be in the second room on the right. Follow me, honey."

I hate being called honey.

As we walked down a narrow, air-conditioned hallway, I found the sweet scent of lavender and soft water sounds alluring. We entered a dimly lit, small, pale blue room with a sheet-draped table set up in the center.

"Sit there." Nicki-with-an-i-not-a-y pointed her pink glittered nail toward the only other piece of furniture, a low stool in the corner. "Javier will be in soon."

I still had all my clothes on and nobody had touched me yet but my heart was speeding like I was being fixed up on a blind date.

My body jerked at the knock on the door. "Come in." My voice high-pitched.

41

"Glad to see you, Suzanne, I'm Javier."

I met the warm hand that was offered. He had a crop of dark, tousled hair, the shadow of a beard and was well muscled in a black t-shirt. "Before we begin, I'd like to know if you have any specific ailments or requests we should discuss." Picking up on my confused expression, he continued, "like lower back pain or a pinched nerve in your neck. How about any areas, shoulders maybe, where you'd like me to concentrate?"

I licked my dry lips. "I've always liked my feet massaged." Looking up into his large brown eyes, I saw him pause.

"Okaaay. Reflexology. That's a start." His broad smile revealed celebrity white teeth that contrasted with his perfectly bronzed skin. He turned, his hand on the doorknob. "I'm going to give you privacy for a few minutes. Please remove your clothes and lie face up on the table with the extra sheet over you."

"For a foot massage? Everything off?"

"Your choice. Leave your underwear on if it makes you feel more comfortable. But just so you know, I use massage oil and it might stain."

"Thanks for the warning," I said under my breath as the door clicked shut.

After I took off my white tank top, denim cut-offs and pink sports bra, leaving on only my black lace thong, I lay on the warm blanketed massage table with the sheet pulled up to my chin.

When Javier returned, he lit several candles and turned on what he called Zen relaxation music while he blended several oils onto his hands. After shutting the door he lifted the lower end of the sheet and held my

feet until they were warm. Slowly kneading the middle
fleshy part on the bottom of each foot, he pulled on my
toes and pushed deep into my arches. I moaned.

Foot massage. An erogenous zone?

"Good," he whispered. "Your sounds tell me your
energy channels have been blocked but are beginning
to release built-up toxins. Have you recently
experienced any trauma?"

"I have PTSD from leaving an alcoholic and
abusive husband."

"I'm so sorry. My parents divorced when I was
young. My father was an alcoholic, too. I understand
how negatively all that affects a person." Javier
sounded sincere, even sympathetic.

I sensed a bonding beginning between us and
could feel his enthusiasm as he worked on certain
spots, explaining how each place on the foot
corresponded to a specific organ or area of the body.
For example, he demonstrated how massaging the toes
helped drain the sinuses.

"Javier, I think I'm ready to go beyond the feet."

I can always say, STOP.

"Good. Turn face down and we'll begin." He
discreetly held up the sheet as I rolled over, then folded
it down to expose my naked back. I flinched when he
put his hands on my shoulders but relaxed as he
stroked downward over the blades, onto either side of
my spine, spending time on my lower back before
working his way back to my shoulders and down
again. "How's the pressure?"

I moaned repeatedly. Guess he took that as
affirmative.

"You're very tight, Suzanne, but some points are

freeing up. Are you ready for me to do your legs?"

"Yes, please," I said politely, keeping my mini turn on to myself.

One leg at a time, Javier kneaded the muscles on the top of my thigh, then downward, lightly circling and rubbing my knee with his fingers. Gently grabbing my calf muscles, he massaged using his thumbs and palms as he gradually worked his way up the side of my leg to the base of my hip. My breath quickened. I tried hard not to squirm but lost the battle. Worse, I had to fight the urge to take his fingers and slide them into the moist opening between my legs.

But Javier ignored my subtle arousal signs and worked my other leg with his same neutral skill set of slow strokes. "Would you like me to do the insides of your thighs?"

Oh man. This is it.

"Please." I whispered. And with one hand reached under the sheet, hooked a thumb over the thin waistband and pulled down my black thong, flipping it to the floor.

WHOOSH!

A blast of chilled air blew in as the door burst open and slammed into the wall behind it. My head snapped up as I heard a voice.

"Hey, honey, is that your green Ford out front blocking the fire lane?"

Chapter Eight ⤨

HEAT RADIATED OFF THE CONCRETE sidewalk as sweat trickled down the sides of my face. Was that why the police felt sorry for me? Or was it the old car I drove, my disoriented look or the need for directions to the nearest Al-Anon meeting? After taking a Breathalyzer test to prove it wasn't an Alcoholic Anonymous meeting I needed, they were nice enough not to give me a ticket. I admitted I was new to the area, and they told me a seven o'clock Al-Anon meeting was two blocks away in the basement of Holy Spirit Church on Woodlawn Avenue.

With two hours to kill, I went to an air-conditioned restaurant with the cute name of Pam's Place in the strip mall and ordered a salad. When I reached in the pocket of my shorts for my wallet to pay the check, my fingers closed around the folded up massage coupon Javier had shoved my way as I ran down that ridiculous circular staircase to move my car.

"For next time," he shouted after me. "A free massage. I didn't finish."

Thanks, Javier. But I'm the one who didn't finish.

WITH TEN MINUTES TO SPARE, I walked into my

first Al-Anon meeting. I scanned the room. Good, no one looked familiar. The tank top and cut-offs I wore stuck to my body just going from the car into the church but I didn't care; I wasn't there to make an impression.

Twenty or so people hugged and chatted before everyone took a seat in a large circle. I was sure I had more problems than anyone—jobless, broke and splitting from a jerk-off named Frank. And oh, yeah, recently ripped from the possibility of an orgasm from Javier. Did that count?

Guidelines of meeting behaviors were read out loud, as well as the Twelve Steps of Al-Anon based on the Twelve Steps of Alcoholics Anonymous. After having an alcoholic for a father, then stupidly marrying another alcoholic, what could they teach me that I didn't know about alcoholism?

The leader, an enthusiastic woman with short, curly red hair, picked a topic for the night: *CHANGE*. Everyone took turns relating their experience of how the disease of alcoholism affected their family and personal life and how they were learning to change.

I listened.

Halfway through the meeting I noticed a quiet woman sitting across from me. She had brown hair pulled back in a ponytail and an attractive, but expressionless, face. Her downcast eyes and tightly folded arms told a story. I knew that story.

After the meeting most people hung around to talk, hug—man, those people were nonstop huggers— and drink coffee. Not me. I headed for the door almost colliding with ponytail woman.

"Is this your first meeting?" I whispered.

"That obvious?"

"I'm a newcomer, too," I said, pushing the door open to the parking lot. "I thought about sharing but I'm not ready to tell my deepest, darkest secrets yet," I said, wondering if she had suffered as much as I had. "Hey, you want to grab a cup of coffee and talk? Just the two of us?"

Ponytail woman's eyes lit up as she stuck out her hand. "Great idea. I'm Leigh."

"Hi, Leigh. I'm Suzanne."

IT TURNED OUT LEIGH WAS VERY TALKATIVE one on one in a back booth in the nearby Courtside Diner. Her hands shook slightly when she picked up her coffee cup and described her drunken husband who lied, cheated and emotionally, and sometimes physically, abused her during the seventeen years of their marriage.

"My marriage," I chimed in, "was really a one-night stand that unfortunately lasted almost seven years. And I also had an alcoholic father. On my wedding night he was so drunk he died in a car wreck—with an oncoming train."

"Oh. My. God. I'm so sorry, Suzanne. It seems we have some things in common. Listen to this." Her voice rose to an alarming level as she spoke. "Both my parents were alcoholics. My father was from Manhattan, the Upper East Side, very handsome, very rich and very strict. Thankfully, I went away to college but my poor mother had to stay home and endure the brunt of my father's alcoholic rages. Her way of dealing was to drink and black out."

47

"So like the hot mess in my home, except my father didn't rage. He was too drunk and went to bed to sleep it off."

"When I was in my early twenties, I married," she said," to get away from the home front."

"Me, too." Right then I shut up. I could tell she needed to finish her story.

"But, no surprise, Fred was just like my father," Leigh continued. "Good-looking but a real shit. A year ago my parents died in a plane crash while on a trip to inspect a winery my father wanted to buy in California. He'd insisted my mother travel with him on our private plane. He was the pilot. And for that, I will never forgive him."

"How absolutely awful!" I reached over and squeezed her hands as our eyes met in mutual understanding.

"I married young to get away from the alcoholic dysfunction in my home, too. But I certainly wasn't going to admit I'd made a mistake marrying another alcoholic and run home. My husband's name is Frank. Another good-looking shit. Well, not so good-looking now."

"Husbands Frank and Fred, Suzanne. It's like we're related by some set of eerie identical happenings!"

"Oddly similar, that's for sure. So why come to Jersey?"

"I'm staying in Pleasant Hill with Aunt Rose, my father's sister. She's the one who suggested I try Al-Anon. She owns the Chesterton Real Estate Agency in a strip mall near here. I have my license and work part time there, and she's helping me sort out my parents' estate. I'm in touch with Fred. I'm sure he's fucking around like always. He's living in our town house in New York City, and when he received papers from the court of my intent to divorce him, wow, was he angry. How about your marriage?"

"Another parallel twist of fate! Before I left where we lived in South Jersey, I told Frank I was divorcing him and going back to my maiden name. Man, he was pissed, too. Now I'm staying at my mother's in Summit about fifteen minutes from here. That reminds me, it's late and I better text her." I laughed. "Almost thirty and still reporting to Mom."

"Yeah, but at least you have a mom to report to."

OUTSIDE WE TRADED PHONE NUMBERS and promised to keep in touch before the next Al-Anon meeting the following week. I figured I'd book an appointment for Massage Time the same afternoon as the meeting but I had a heart shift. "Leigh, here's something to help you relax." I reached in my pocket and handed her the coupon for a free massage. "Ask for Javier."

"Oh yeah, I know this place. It's at the end of the strip mall where my real estate office is located in Pleasant Hill. You're the best, Suzanne," she said, giving me a hug before she got into her car. "In many ways we're sisters of sorrow."

Sisters of sorrow. I shivered in spite of the heat.

MOM WAS SO THRILLED TO HEAR I went to an Al-Anon meeting she hardly asked about Massage Time. I did tell her the stuff about Evelyn quitting, the ditzy

49

receptionist and the place being up for sale. I glossed over the massage part, saying it was relaxing but too short because I had to move the car.

"Don't forget, Suzanne, I bought a whole book of coupons and you're welcome to all of them. But remember, next time *park in the back!"*

"It's late, but tomorrow I'll tell you all about Al-Anon."

"I can't wait to hear. One question: Was it a discussion or a topic meeting?"

"The topic was *CHANGE.*"

"If that's the case, that dragonfly that had you in its sights the other night certainly has psychic powers."

I laughed. "You've done a major Jedi Mind Trick on me about that dragonfly, Mom."

"Seriously, Suzanne, I did a bit more research and took notes on the back of a magazine." She sorted through the stack of miscellaneous papers and magazines on the coffee table. "Ah, here it is. It seems everywhere in the world the dragonfly symbolizes *change* regarding self-realization, mental and emotional maturity and the ability to understand the deeper meaning of life."

"Whoa. Deeper meaning of life. Me?"

"I think that means you can have fun but don't persist in meaningless or harmful tasks and activities. Your quest must be to find out what is *your* passion, *your* purpose, what makes *your* heart sing. Then go for it."

"Did you get that from Al-Anon or a fortune cookie—or a blue bug with four wings?"

"No, from *online* research. Seriously, look at my life since your dad died. Can't you see how I've grown? How I've changed? Starting with how I eat. Less ooey-gooey pancakes and more good proteins and vegetables. And tomorrow I'll tell you how Buddy and I got certified and now volunteer at the children's hospital twice a week to share our love with others through animal therapy. It's the first time I ever did anything meaningful in my life, except for raising you."

I smiled and nodded. "But you always seemed such a natural at it all when I was growing up. Well, except for those endless, demanding lists of yours!"

"Let me tell you change was hard at first. I was set in my ways. Certain times for meals and TV programs, certain clothes, certain friends, and a certain way of thinking. But, ever so slowly, I began to see there was more to life. Much, much more. It's a heavy subject," she said, covering a yawn, "and I'm really sleepy. We'll talk tomorrow. Love you, sweetie." She kissed my forehead and turned.

I watched as she walked down the hall to her bedroom, Buddy following a few steps behind.

"Goodnight, Mom," I yelled after her. "Love you, too."

FINALLY!

I sprinted upstairs, remembering my afternoon arousal-lite and my desire to finish what had begun at Massage Time. I wondered if Javier felt as stimulated giving the massage as I felt receiving it. I pictured his powerful arms and hard muscular body and wondered what his dick looked like, felt like, tasted like. My hand closed around my vibrator as I grabbed it out of the drawer of my night table. And stopped.

No. Not tonight.

Today I experienced the real thing. Real, satisfying human touch. Now I wanted a slow, lingering massage, to be hypnotized by the build-up of stimulation stroke after stroke, and the absolute certainty that I didn't need to pretend, respond or reciprocate: only enjoy. This time I didn't want to do anything. This time I wanted to be done.

Chapter Nine ✕

Sleep wasn't happening. Desperate for a distraction from thinking about Javier and my no-go getting off, I thought maybe a little light reading would help. Kneeling to search in the lower shelf of my bookcase, I ran my finger along the titles of a few classics my mother made me keep: *Charlotte's Web, Dr. Dolittle, The Magic Garden* and all the Nancy Drew and Judy Blume books. Next to them stood our family's faded and falling apart dictionary. Wait, what was that sex term Julia used? Flipping through the pages, I found it: optical illusion—visually perceived objects and images that differ from reality.

I don't get it. How was that a sex term?

It was eleven-thirty. I knew Julia was just finishing up the nighttime liquor inventory at Dr. Unk's. Tapping on her number in my phone directory, the call went through. I propped up the bed pillows behind me, leaned back and waited.

"Suzanne, so good to hear from you. I miss you."

"And I really miss you, too, Julia. Listen, I hate to be a pain in the ass at this time of night but I've got a quick sex question. What's the deal with the optical illusion?"

53

"Well, we're all suckers for a good magic trick. And the secret to them all is *misdirection* and *misperception!*" She laughed a nervous laugh. "But we'll discuss that later. I've got more important things to tell you. Jerry's thinking about quitting the bar."

"What? He'd never do that! He's married to Dr. Unk's."

"I didn't have to hire Sherlock Holmes to realize Jerry's decision had something to do with you leaving."

"Me? He hardly even noticed me when I was there. Last time I spoke to him he was borderline nasty. Wait, scratch borderline. Just plain nasty's more like it."

"Frankly, Suzanne, I don't think he's ever gotten over you. Years ago when he heard you moved to South Jersey with your new husband, he threw himself deeper into the bar business and never came up for air."

"Uh huh. And for all those years he took out all his anguish and despair by sucking and fucking all his female employees."

And at Dr. Unks I felt unloved, unwanted and uneverything.

"I'll admit he used sex as Novocain. It worked— for a while. Then you showed up."

"Julia, that's ridiculous."

"Have I ever lied to you?"

"No. But this—"

"I'm no Dr. Sigmund Freud but he hasn't been acting like himself. A few nights ago I asked him what was wrong. He seemed to want to say something, needed to say something. After hesitating he blurted out, 'I fell in love with Suzanne in ninth grade math class, and I've been falling ever since.'"

I swallowed, my mouth suddenly dry. The truth of what she said struck me silent.

"Suzanne, it was like a door opening a crack. I got a glimpse of the real Jerry inside. No guardrails, no cover-ups." Julia did have the gift of getting right through people's bullshit. "I waited for more but he got quiet and went into the kitchen."

"None of it matters now, Julia. None of it."

But it did.

"Thank you for telling me about Jerry." I dug deep for my long muted internal voice. "But I swore after allowing my douchebag ex-husband to treat me like dirt I would never, ever, let anyone do that to me again."

"But you're the one who left Jerry first—for Frank. Remember, Suzanne?"

I wanted to tell her she was wrong but I didn't because she wasn't.

"Yes, but he adjusted."

"Maybe not."

After she gave me several more bits of advice, we said our goodbyes, I flattened my bed pillows, rolled over and thought about Julia's last words: "Soften your heart, Suzanne." I pictured Jerry's face and remembered how he looked at me, touched me, talked to me. I could feel my eyelids flutter and when I finally closed them heard an inner voice that sounded a lot like my own.

A wrong turn is not a dead end.

THE NEXT MORNING I GLANCED at the clock on the night table: 10 a.m. Usually I was up much earlier, but last night's convoluted conversation with Julia invaded my dreams as I must have unconsciously tried to sort out the facts as I slept. It reminded me of the fairy tale, *The Princess and the Pea*. Forget the annoyance of sleeping on one pea. I must have slept the night on an entire bag.

After sweating out a half an hour in the shower with the temperature up to the max, I switched to cold for a few minutes and woke up. No green smoothie today. I wanted pancakes—with real maple syrup!

AS I ATE, MOM WATCHED. "I won't make a habit of all these carbs, but just this once can't hurt," I told her. "Later, I thought I'd go for a run to burn off the calories. See it all equals out."

She smiled. "I'm glad to see you so happy. Now tell me more about the Al-Anon meeting."

"It was really informative. And I had coffee with a newcomer afterward. Hope you don't mind, but I gave her one of your massage coupons. She looked like she needed it."

"Perfect, Suzanne. Only one meeting and you're already doing service. *Service.* That's one of the tools of a recovery program, you know."

"Yes, they talked about practicing service to others and self-care to ourselves, too. So after I go running, I think I may get a massage. A complete one this time, with nothing missing."

"You better call soon and make an appointment if you want the same person you had last time."

I panicked and grabbed my phone. "Nicki. Two o'clock, Javier?" My breath caught for a moment. "All set? Good. Thanks." I exhaled as I hung up.

This girl's going to have a little "me" time today. Yeah, right. Me and Javier.

Chapter Ten ✕

I SAT FIDDLING WITH MY HANDS in the light blue, gently lit room waiting for a ninety-minute, full body, deep tissue massage. I knew what to expect but still quivered from nervous adrenaline as momentary thoughts of canceling crossed my mind. The door opened, and I couldn't help but smile when Javier entered the room. He returned an even wider smile. Interesting, there was a sense of calm in his dark brown eyes as they met mine.

"Good to see you, Suzanne. I'm happy you're here for a full massage after last time—with no interruptions."

"Yes, I parked in the back. I'm a fast learner."

He chuckled. "Well, now you know the *full* drill," he said as he excused himself and shouldered the door to leave. "You can disrobe, and when I come back in, we'll begin."

There wasn't much clothing to take off this time because I wore no underwear. I love going commando. It makes me feel like I have a secret. I lay face up on the warm massage table and pulled the extra sheet up, covering my naked body.

Javier knocked and, after my affirmative response,

reentered. He dimmed the lights, lowered the New Age spa music and rubbed oil on his hands and muscular arms. Then, facing me, he spoke in a somewhat whispered tone. "As you know, I will ask you if you are in agreement each time *before* I move to a different part of the body." With penetrating eye contact, he continued, "Also as we proceed, I will want to know if you have any boundaries. Please be open and honest. I am not here to judge you, only to please you."

Please me? No man ever wanted to just please me.

Javier asked me to flip facedown. Too bad. Couldn't see his handsome face that way but the warmth of the massage table on my chest and stomach made me feel comforted and at ease. Folding the sheet to the back of my knees, he put an additional hand towel over my glutes.

Beginning with long, leisurely strokes from the bottom of my back moving upward, he explained the importance of going with the blood flow to the heart. While at the top, Javier massaged my shoulders and neck, periodically reminding me to take deep, slow breaths to encourage relaxation. Repeating the pattern of up from the lower back over the blades, then down the sides was hypnotic and increasing the pressure, he said, and would warm up the back muscles. Up and down, back up and down, soon I felt time had stopped and I was drifting in space.

"I'm going to do your legs next," Javier said in a low voice.

"Yes," I mumbled in agreement.

I never felt any transition but I did hear him reapplying coconut oil to his hands, then gently cupping and palming my calves and tracing his fingers down to my ankles. Massaging my legs felt so good, especially after my morning run, until he asked a question.

"Thighs next, Suzanne?"

"Please," I murmured from some outer worldly zone.

After several more long strokes up and down my legs, Javier worked the backs of my thighs.

I moaned.

"The tension in your tendons is finally releasing. Would you like me to do the insides of your thighs?"

"Oh, yes," my voice throaty. I was getting beyond the point of no return and ready for the session to take a sensual turn. Panting and grabbing the edges of the sheet, I was balling up the material over and over, then releasing my fists. Did Javier notice?

"Remember," he whispered, "no one's judging you here. Let everything go."

With his palms and thumbs massaging the backs of my thighs, I thought I was going to come any second. So crazy, I have only ever climaxed with my vibrator. I tried to slow the feeling but now my hips were grinding up and down without my permission. When his hands went in between my thighs, my breathing increased as he got nearer and nearer to the throbbing between my legs. Suddenly, I exploded, convulsing nonstop.

When I came down to a seminormal state, embarrassment took over. "I'm sorry, but I think I'm done."

"No, you're not. You've got a lot more to let go. But if you want to stop now, it's okay. This is new for you, am I right?"

"Yes. New." I pulled the sheet up around me and sat up. "But I feel great—maybe a little sleepy."

"A very common reaction, Suzanne. It was my pleasure to see you again, but when you come back, we will do some other things you might enjoy. However, please remember: What happens at Massage Time stays at Massage Time."

"Got it," I said, putting a finger to my lips. "The secret's safe with me."

WALKING TO MY VW VAN, I felt a little off balance, almost woozy. I drove out and fit myself into a space in the adjacent back parking lot of Chesterton Realty. I killed the engine and sat, trying to work up the energy to drop in and say hello to Leigh. But, what was that noise? Turning my head, I saw Leigh's face peering in and tap-tapping on the glass. I rolled down the window.

"Hey, Leigh, I didn't think you'd recognize my van. I just got a massage at two o'clock. Did you make an appointment yet?"

"I knew it was you. You told me you had a '67 VW bus. Remember? My massage time is tomorrow at three o'clock. Want to get some coffee now?"

"No, thanks. I'm beat. But call me after your session with Javier and we'll talk. Anyway, I'll see you at the Al-Anon meeting next week. Sound good?"

We shook hands through the window, and I drove out of the parking lot. I wanted to stop, go in the back of the van and take a nap. But it was getting late, and I needed to get on the road before the traffic built up. Man, that massage wore me out.

At home Mom was busy sweeping leaves off the patio. Buddy dove into every pile, barking like crazy as he burst out, danced around and dashed into the next nearby stack.

"Hi, Mom," I called out the sliding glass door as I watched the endearing scene. "Going upstairs to take a little nap before dinner. Okay?"

"No problem, sweetie. It's a casual night. I ordered out from Courtside Diner. They'll deliver in at six."

Upstairs I flopped onto my bed, thought about Javier for two minutes and felt myself drifting off. The next thing I knew Mom was yelling from downstairs. "Almost dinnertime, Suzanne."

I looked in the bathroom mirror. Yikes, messy massage-head! I decided it was ponytail time and dabbed on some lipstick. Denim capris, my red tank top and a chambray shirt tied at the waist completed the outfit. While running downstairs I heard Mom call out from the kitchen, "Please answer the door, Suzanne, it's the food delivery."

I had rubbed my favorite Lily of the Valley lotion on my hands and had trouble negotiating the locks on the front door. Mom was a big locker-upper. A North Jersey thing. Finally, my slippery fingers twisted and turned the knobs, and the door opened a crack. I stumbled back and stopped short.

"Oh. My. God. Jerry?"

Chapter Eleven ⊁

"GREAT. JUST FUCKING GREAT."

"Wait, Suz, don't shut me out," Jerry said, yanking the handle of the door toward him while I pulled back on the inside knob. "Guess you're not going to invite me in."

With my other hand I gripped the doorsill to steady myself and stared as anger rose. "Not likely."

"I'm here to tell you I'm sorry."

"Sorry about what?"

"You. Me. Everything."

"Uh huh."

"I've been thinking about us a lot lately."

My body stiffened. "What about us?"

"All I know is the bar lost its appeal when you left."

"Yeah, right," I said, noticing how his deep blue eyes were not leaving my face as he stood framed in the now open doorway. "What about all the dancers you slept your way through?"

"You're being sarcastic but I'm being serious."

"I'm not being sarcastic. I'm being honest. Well, what *do you* want, Jerry?"

Oh man, he's still so damn sexy in those jeans.

"For starters, I need to find a job up here in North Jersey."

"I never thought you'd be coming back."

"Neither did I."

After my talk with Julia, my heart wanted to believe what Jerry was telling me, but my head hadn't gotten the memo. She was right about one thing. Who *was* the real Jerry? I had no idea.

"You're flip-flopping all over the place. North, south, middle and back again. How do I know this isn't another flip? Or flop?"

His lips curled upwards in a slight smile. *A smile that shot right through me.*

"I hope it won't be a flop. But I'd like to see you. Lunch, dinner, coffee? Please, so we can talk without having a 'tug of door' between us."

His eyes were clear and penetrating but never betraying his inner thoughts.

Working hard to keep control of my mouth and facial expressions, I said, "My best days now are the ones when I don't think of you. It's a dead end, Jerry." And I shoved the front door shut with a resounding bang.

Did I want to spend time leading him on? No. Most of all I didn't want to lead myself on. Again.

"WHERE'S THE FOOD?" Mom asked as she rounded the corner from the kitchen.

"It's not here yet, Mom. That was Jerry."

"Jerry? Your Jerry?"

"Not *my* Jerry. But yes, Jerry Spinella."

"What happened?"

"Long story short, he's quitting the bar scene, moving north and wants to see me."

"How nice and flattering, Suzanne. Don't you want to see him? You used to adore him."

"I still do. But that's another story for another time," I said, opening the door for the kid with the food delivery.

"SHALL WE EAT INSIDE OR OUT?" Mom asked.

"You just swept the patio. Let's eat outside."

Buddy kept us entertained by rolling in the grass and catching tennis balls we threw to him. How could we not throw them back into the yard when he so dutifully returned the balls and placed them at our feet, his eyes so hopeful? The slimier they got, the more he wanted us to toss them one—more—time.

"If you don't want to talk about Jerry, then explain to me exactly what happened between you and Frank?"

Now that I was staying in Mom's house, she deserved to hear at least part of that story. "You know, the usual stuff in a marriage with an alcoholic and drug addict. I basically survived by not thinking and not feeling. It's difficult to talk about because I've been trying hard to outrun the memories. But you're looking at the biggest fool that ever lived."

"I couldn't figure out why you stayed with him for so long. You hinted he was sometimes verbally abusive. Why didn't you just come home?" she said as she moved to the large swing seat on the edge of the patio.

Buddy, taking his cue, jumped into her lap.

We laughed at Buddy's surprise leap. "Coincidentally, Mom, it's all about a dog."

"What dog? You never said you had a dog."

"I didn't want to tell you because I wanted to handle it myself," I said, playing with my shirttails. "And I did."

"Get to the part about the dog, Suzanne," she said, balancing on the edge of the swing."And don't leave anything out."

"As payment for work he did on a car, Frank accepted a five-year-old dog in return. A couple was moving to a small apartment and couldn't take their German shepherd. Frank thought he could train it to be a guard dog for his auto body shop because some expensive tools had been taken during several local robberies. He thought the dog, Gunner, looked scary and mean because he was huge. Really huge. Frank told me he renamed it Gun Shot, thinking the name would sound more threatening to thieves."

"Was Frank nice to the dog?" A typical question from Mom, the champion for all animals.

"Neglectful is a better word because he was usually stoned or drunk."

"I'm not liking this story. If you had just told me," she leaned in closer, "I would have come down immediately and brought you and the dog home."

"Relax, Mom. The story has a good ending," I said as she settled back in her seat.

"Tell me."

"When I saw the dog for the first time at the garage, something happened. He looked into my eyes for a long time, and at that moment I felt I'd known him forever. It was a look that went all the way to my heart. I knew then I had to rescue Gun Shot from a life of just lying on a cement floor in an auto body shop. I told Frank I was going to take him home and train him myself. Frank was too boozed up and out of it to care."

"Did you take him through a guard dog training course?"

"No way. This 125-pound dog was no guard dog. Gun Shot was a lap dog. Every day we'd run or take a long walk, then he'd sit by me with his head resting on my knees as I read or watched TV. When Frank would come home, Gun Shot, who I renamed Gunny, would give out a low growl. Frank would curse, go into the bedroom and black out. Before he left for work the next day, he'd searched for the bottle he misplaced the night before. Gunny would quietly position himself beside me, snarl and bare his teeth, and Frank would run out slamming the door behind him.

It didn't matter. Nothing mattered. Except Gunny.

"So the dog, without being physically aggressive, protected you from Frank."

"Exactly, Mom. But somehow I got an insight from that dog. There was no one coming to save me. I was the one who had to save myself. "

"That's wonderful but where's Gunny now?"

"He died about two months ago of bone cancer. I had to put him to sleep to end his suffering. The hardest thing I ever had to do."

Rest in peace, dear Gunny. Rest in peace.

"I'm so sorry, Suzanne."

"Me, too, Mom. Now I like to remember him running through the woods ahead of me. He'd bark and chase the squirrels off the path so I wouldn't trip." Tears that had collected leaked down the sides of my face. More kept coming. I let them flow.

"So that's why you stayed with Frank for several years longer than necessary. To take care of Gunny."

"Had to, Mom. Had to. I loved that dog. He gave me his all."

"From what I've heard and read about this phenomenon, Gunny wasn't really a dog."

Raising my eyes, I sat back.

"He was a spirit guide in a dog's body. He came to you just at the time you needed him because you were living in a combat zone with an addict."

"Do you think so, Mom?"

"I know so, Suzanne," she said, stroking Buddy's head. "I know so."

"HEY, MOM, THOSE BIG SALADS from the Courtside Diner were delicious, but let's not go inside yet. How about we stay outside for a little bit and see if that pesky dragonfly will show up?"

"Not pesky, *interesting*. I put new wood in the fire pit so we're good to go." She leaned down and struck the matches, lighting the dry kindling in the center first. "I think the fire will attract the bugs and make them easier for us to see."

Rubbing my hands together, I squatted beside the wrought iron pit to warm myself. Rising to get more twigs, I came face to face with the dragonfly.

"Don't move," Mom warned. "You'll scare it away."

"But I don't want it to bite me."

"I don't think they bite. She just wants to get to know you."

"She? How do you know it's a she?"

"I don't. I'm guessing. I think males would be out searching for food or females, not making friends with

68

humans," Mom said, taking her phone out of the pocket of her slacks. "Yesterday I got some scientific dragonfly info. Listen to this. Meanwhile, keep still."

I stood statue-like while Mom read from her phone. I thought the dragonfly would dart away but now it was circling, going backward, diving and pulling up in front of my face as if it were showing me its best tricks.

"The nymph, in the beginning of the life cycle of the dragonfly, emerges from the egg after spending up to five years beneath the water's surface. When it is ready to metamorphosis into an adult, it splits its old larval skin, crawls out and waits for the sun to rise. Then, pumping up its newly dried wings, it flies off to find a mate and lay her eggs, living only for a few months."

"What?" Five years under water, then a few months in the air? That's no life."

"Shhh. No judgments. It'll hear you. Supposedly," she continued, "around the world this style of life symbolizes not only accepting change but also the virtue of living in the moment and to the fullest. That way you are aware of who you are, where you are, what you want, what you don't and can make informed choices on a moment-to-moment basis."

"Got it." I whispered to the dragonfly, going along with Mom's playbook of talking to bugs like they were people. Then, putting my hand over my heart, I pledged: "I promise I will try to live in the present moment and be willing to investigate first in order to make smart choices. And, oh, I will use failures as opportunities for change."

As if satisfied, it hovered in front of my face for a

few seconds longer, then flitted away. Just in case it really understood, I silently mouthed, "Thank You."

Chapter Twelve ⊁

"OKAY, LEIGH, SO ON A SCALE FROM 1 to 10, 10 being the best, how did you like the massage?"

Leigh had texted me to say the massage she received that afternoon was fabulous but she needed to talk.

I bet she did.

I got us a back table for privacy at Pam's Place and couldn't wait to hear her answer. Hesitating at first, she finally spoke. "Hmm, I'd give it a 12. No, 23. Wait, 42. Final answer 75 or perhaps even an 85!"

I was laughing so hard I almost peed in my jeans and excused myself to go to the ladies room. Still laughing, I came back to my seat. Leigh was laughing at my laughter when the waitress, Sally, brought our Greek salads.

She eyeballed us, "That must have been *some* joke."

"No joke," I came back. "We were discussing women's orgasms."

"Well, if there's any to be had," she lowered her voice, "please let me know."

"Sally, you'll be first on the list," Leigh stated.

"Please, God," Sally said under her breath as she turned and went back behind the counter.

We munched as we talked nonstop, heaping praise on Javier for his massage techniques leading to an unforgettable climax.

"What did you like best?" I blurted out before I could stop myself.

"His unbelievably strong and knowing hands. The strokes were so sensual, even if he was just massaging my arm." Her unfocused eyes seemed in a far-off zone. Seconds later, she shook her head, returning her conscious mind back from her own alternate reality. "And the fact that I didn't have to do a *fucking thing*. Wasn't that glorious?"

"The best!" I said, glancing around to see if anyone was listening. "All this sex talk makes me want another massage. How about you?" I whispered to Leigh.

"You've got to be kidding. Every day, like brushing my teeth."

"But seriously," I asked, "*why do you think* Javier wants to give women orgasms?"

"Maybe he feels sorry for us. You know, divorces, cheating husbands, addictions, neglect, money issues, et cetera, et cetera."

"Maybe he's gay," I offered up and quickly took it back.

"Maybe it's basically a turn on," she smirked, "looking and touching naked women. But then, why would he want to make a dozen appointments a day? How much turning on does one man need? Or, could it be simply about bigger tips."

"Maybe it's a combination of all those things. Nevertheless, it's very odd, and I don't get it. But I'm going to find out!"

"I want to know, too, Suzanne, but meanwhile, I'm worried Javier might lose his license. We won't tell but some uptight ladies might. Then the place would get raided and he'd be arrested."

"And we'd be out of luck," I frowned. "But wait a freakin' minute. What about men getting a happy ending? Why aren't they all hauled into court? Something's not right or fair. You know, Leigh, this is a *serious* problem with plenty of questions and no answers. I'm going to call Massage Time right now, make an appointment with Javier and find out what's really going on there."

At that point we both fell into uncontrolled laughter, knowing what I really wanted was an excuse to have another massage. I punched in the number on my phone.

"It's five o'clock, Suzanne. They're probably closed."

"Wait, somebody picked up. Hello, Javier? It's Suzanne Quinlan. Hey, how come you're answering the phone? What, Nicki quit? Oh, man, I'm sorry to hear that. Is the owner going to take over? No? What? Do I want a job? Are you kidding? Short term? How short? A few weeks. Well, I guess I could. Okay, see you at 9:30 tomorrow. You're very welcome. It will be my pleasure. Yes, I'll think of a few ways you can pay me back."

"I can't believe you made a two-minute phone call and got a job—with benefits!"

"Don't make me laugh or I really might pee in my pants this time."

"Suzanne, the day I met you was my lucky day."

"Backatcha, babe."

I GOT HOME AT ELEVEN, AWARE I needed to be up early. Tiptoeing inside, I didn't want to wake Mom.

"Suzanne, is that you?"

"Sorry if I woke you."

"I'm in the living room. How was your dinner? Did you have a good time?"

"All good, Mom. I'm going up to bed."

"Come in for a minute. I need to tell you something."

"What's up, Mom?"

She was sitting silently in the corner of the couch. There was no TV on, her hands were folded in her lap and her face was sealed in a mask of concern—a mask familiar to me all the years I lived in this house.

"Uh oh, what's wrong? Has Jerry been back annoying you?"

"No, dear. It's just that, well, you know that I'm in Al-Anon and part of my recovery is to make amends." She put her hand up just as I was opening my mouth. "Let me continue before I lose my nerve."

"Okay, Mom. But you are a great mom."

"Thank you, sweetie. Well, here we go," she said as she took out a piece of paper from a pocket of her bathrobe. "As I progressed in the program, I had to look at all the relationships I've had. I began to realize I had a part in all the problems."

"But you weren't the alcoholic."

"Yes, but I felt responsible for Dad's behavior, your growing up without a functioning father and for trying to hide our difficulties from the world. I told so many lies trying to protect Dad's and our family's

74

reputation. You were an only daughter of an only daughter who was frustrated and knew nothing about child rearing. You didn't understand my periods of internalized resentment. I learned it's called *silent violence* because my anger inside not only hurt me but also those around me."

"Whoa, Mom, can't we discuss this later?"

"No. This won't be as bad as you imagine, and I need to get it done so I can grow up myself."

"But you have grown. All that healthy food and training Buddy to be a therapy dog."

"There's more to do. Much more. Alcoholism is a family disease, and the making of amends can help free me of the shame and guilt I've felt for perpetuating the pretense of a perfect home when I knew it wasn't. And for putting you under pressure to go along with my ridiculous charade. It's no excuse but maybe at some point you'll come to an understanding for yourself."

"I think I've had plenty of understanding about me from that dragonfly."

We both laughed. "That's true. Seriously, though, I want you to know I am so, so sorry for all the list-making and insisting you carry out all my directives. Somehow I thought organization would be the answer. If your dad was sleeping off a binge, at least we could carry on in an organized fashion. But somehow you got lost in all my pride and selfishness, and I robbed you of your own discoveries, your own growing up. And I'm sorry, too, these last years had to be with Frank, another alcoholic. I can't give you back your early years but I can make *living* amends during all your future years."

"Explain that."

"It means I'm going to change my ways. I'm not going to be in such a rush to accomplish tasks and ignore *you*. And as close as I am to you, as much as I love you, I am not going to try to live your life *for* you. So I'm freeing you from *my* anxiety, from *my* personal idea of what constitutes happiness for you, and I promise to refrain from imposing my will or green smoothies on you. In fact, to show you my heart's in the right place, I'll make you French toast in the morning."

"Well, let's do it early because I just got a new job. And PS: I now love your green smoothies. But back to your amends, I love you and forgive you, Mom. I know you were just trying to do the best you could under tough circumstances."

"Thank you, sweetheart, but did you say job? How did that happen? I thought you were only going to dinner."

"Well, while Leigh and I were eating in Pam's Place, I called Massage Time to book an appointment for next week. I found out Nicki the receptionist quit so I was offered that job on a temporary basis. Exciting, huh?"

"Very! And such a nice atmosphere. Good for you, Suzanne. Okay, you better get to bed; I'll rustle up that French toast in the morning. And thank you again for being so gracious and kind while I made my amends."

"Well since I'm in Al-Anon now, will you be understanding when I have to make mine to you?"

"You can count on it."

Dragonfly Girl

THE NEXT MORNING I OPENED my eyes and realized not only did I have a job but I also forgot to set the alarm. Thank goodness it was only 4:45 a.m. This working thing was going to take practice. A glance out the window revealed a dark sky but a glimmer of light predicted dawn was coming. I reached for my phone on the night table. The weather app indicated it was already 73 degrees with a nasty Jersey dew point on the way. Humidity and tomatoes, that's what we're famous for. Too bad we can't have one without the other. I lay back and grinned to myself, thinking about this state that I loved. There was so much good in New Jersey. Number one, we Jersey girls never, ever, have to pump our own gas, unless we want to. And, of course, George Washington slept here. Above all else, there's miles and miles of boardwalks and beautiful sandcastle-worthy beaches along the ocean. And plenty of mountains to hike and ski and pristine lakes for swimming and boating further inland in this our Garden State.

And oh, I can't forget, Jerry Spinella, a real Jersey Boy, born and raised. I wondered if I should give him another chance—probably to be hurt again. But I did promise the dragonfly I would investigate first before making a decision. For today, however, while I'm at Massage Time, Jerry would be on the back burner. Some other intriguing things there had jumped to the front.

Chapter Thirteen ⊀

I PARKED IN THE BACK AND SAT for a moment with my palms and forehead resting on the steering wheel before entering Massage Time. It wasn't like I was falling in love with Javier, but, oh man, I enjoyed sneaking a peek at the muscles rippling underneath his t-shirt, his category five smile and a curl of his thick, black hair falling down as he massaged my body and brought me to a climax.

Get a grip, Suzanne.

Embarrassed by my own thoughts, I entered the building. Rather than negotiating the circular staircase, I faced the dragonfly wallpaper in the lobby, searched and found the UP button and pressed it to take the elevator. While riding to the second floor, I noticed the theme carried out with dragonfly images on a border of the same wallpaper along the top of the inside of the elevator. *Okay, okay, I remember your messages: Stay in the moment, welcome change and investigate before decision-making*, I silently declared, hoping the dragonfly at home in Summit was adept at mental telepathy, thought transference, ESP or good, old-fashioned mind reading from here in Pleasant Hill.

"Hi, Javier." I called out nervously as I pushed my

way through the big glass doors with chrome handles. "It's Suzanne. I'm here."

"Give me a minute. Have a seat."

Sitting behind the long wooden desk where Nicki once sat, I picked up a magazine and started to thumb through until I realized I was reading articles without paying attention, thinking only of Javier and his magic hands.

"Suzanne, sorry to keep you waiting," Javier said, coming out from one of the massage rooms down the hall.

"Hi, there." Even though I'd seen him twice before, I got a jolt of arousal at the sight of him. "I'm ready to begin."

"I thought I'd give you a brief rundown of your duties, then I'll explain my purpose in doing holistic therapy work while giving you an appreciation massage. I'm so grateful you took this job. There's no way I could schedule appointments on the phone and do massages, too."

"I'm glad I could help, Javier. And there's no way I'd turn down your generous offer of a massage but don't you have any other sessions scheduled?"

"Nothing until noon. So okay, let's get started." Javier sat on the edge of the desk looking down at me in the receptionist chair. He pointed out the desk phones, appointment calendars, towels and oils. Then, indicating the massage rooms down the hall, he spoke about cleaning, sanitizing and getting them ready for the next client.

"And one more thing—"

While he talked I really looked at him. He had a sensual body with smooth olive skin and muscular shoulders; his forehead was slightly slick with sweat, looking as if he'd just come from the gym. My breath quickened just thinking about what was coming next as Javier abruptly turned toward me. Caught! Like peeking inside the boy's locker room in middle school.

His eyes narrowed down on me. "Do you think you can handle the desk work and all the other tasks?"

"Certainly. The phone calls and scheduling seem easy, and nothing too hard about keeping the towels and sheets washed and folded, the massage tables changed and sanitized and the oils inventoried and ordered."

"Great. I just thought you looked a little spaced out. Like the heat had gotten to you."

"Well, er, yes," I said with a nervous laugh, putting a stray hair behind my ear. "I was thinking I could lose at least three pounds of water weight in this climate just walking from the car into the building."

"No, don't lose any weight. Well, maybe just a little bit," he said, putting his thumb and forefinger a half an inch apart in front of my face.

"What did you say?" I said, thinking I looked really hot in the mirror this morning in my short, red print sundress.

"Just kidding. You're perfect."

"Watch it, Javier, the world is hard on women. Starting as girls, most of us never felt pretty enough or thin enough."

"Fair enough." he said sheepishly.

I crossed my arms. "You said there was one more thing you wanted to mention about the job."

"Yes, it has to do with the scheduling. It can get a little dicey. Women want what they want. You can't blame them. So your best bet is to get to know each one. Chat them up when they come in and are waiting. Get to know the names of their kids and husbands, everything about their jobs and hobbies and, most of all, their gripes. Previous personal attention and knowledge are the best hedge against future complaints. In other words, be their friend. Of all the things I've told you, this is the most important."

JAVIER LEFT THE LAVENDER scented room while I changed into *absolutely nothing*. After getting under the top sheet on the massage table facedown, he returned and lowered the relaxing Zen music and, from what I could hear, oiled his hands and arms.

"The massage I'm giving you today will be a little different. I'm going to talk through several parts so you will understand my purpose in what I do, how I do it and why I do it."

"Sort of like a learning lesson?"

"Yes. But I don't want you to be distracted by my talking from feeling all your natural sensations."

Folding the sheet down to the back of my knees, he didn't cover my glutes this time. He started with long, luxurious strokes going from my lower back to my shoulders, then down the sides of my back. He repeated this sequence again and again.

"I am massaging your fascia, the protective layer of soft tissue between your skin and muscle."

I felt a calm but sensual tingling begin to heat up between my legs.

"Your tension level has lessened," he whispered. "Excellent for your general health. Now do you want your glutes massaged? There can be a lot of tension stored in those muscles."

"Please," I uttered.

Javier spent time on my butt and hips and commented on sensing the tension release as he worked his magical powers. I began breathing heavily, repressing moaning and grunting. Nothing fooled Javier.

"Let out your body sounds. Don't keep them in. They get stuck inside, masking as fear and embarrassment. This is all about releasing accumulated stress."

Thank goodness the massage rooms were soundproofed.

"You're doing very well, Suzanne. Your muscles are giving up their stored toxins more easily now. Are you ready for thighs?"

"Yes," I murmured as the need to know Javier's motives was fading.

Slowly, and what seemed lovingly, he moved his hands, fingers and palms in a circular fashion up and down my upper legs.

"What I'm giving you here is a deeper tissue massage to get rid of all the tight knots in your muscles you've accumulated over time."

The growing tingles in my clit were now at throbbing level. I pressed my legs together before I got any wetter.

"Allow yourself to be fully present to your body, its physical feelings and happenings. Let go of anything you are suppressing."

Javier's low voice penetrated my self-consciousness as I unclenched my upper legs, allowing him to trail his fingers along the crease between my butt and leg, then move to my inner thighs, gently gripping and squeezing each thigh. It was as if electricity passed through my entire body landing exactly where X marks the spot.

"If you can roll onto your back, we can do your stomach and chest."

"Oh, yes, please." I accomplished the flip as quickly as I could to continue all the intense sensations.

The stomach massage was made up of unending strokes using both hands, alternately reaching from the near side across the stomach to the far side. Back and forth, then reversed, his rhythm tender, almost loving like a warm hug. I imagined it was Javier's way of making me feel accepted in all ways. As he continued, his hands swept higher and higher.

"Now I'm going to do your upper body including your chest," he whispered. "I sense you're relaxed and ready."

I nodded. No words, no thinking, only Javier's touch.

A figure eight massage around my breasts was a bit heart stopping until I became comfortable with the circular path of his hands. Inching closer to my nipples, Javier said exactly what he was going to do as he began to lightly pinch and roll each one between his fingers. I was squirming, beyond the point of no return, and had to once again squeeze my legs together to stop the pulsing. "Stay loose in your pelvic area, Suzanne, with tension comes numbness. Do you want me to find your G-spot now and help you reach your climax?"

I must have looked confused.

"Most women don't know how to find the G-spot, the K-spot or the A-spot," he said, explaining softly. "Today, we'll start with the easiest, the G-spot. I'll talk you through. My fingers are now circling your pubic area and gradually slipping into your vagina passed the lips and folds of flesh to find the small spongy area on the front internal wall. I will massage this spot with one hand."

Honestly, it wasn't doing much for me.

"While I stimulate your clitoris with the other, reposition yourself anyway that feels good on my fingers and hand. We are partners in your orgasm."

Now you're talkin'! Oh, God. Take me higher and higher. Stop but don't stop. It's too much but I want more, more, more.

"There you go, Suzanne. Take it all in. Be captured by your feelings. Free your mind, your body, your soul."

My back was arching, my hips bucking and my legs quivering as my sensitive clit and the walls of my vagina were shuddering and pulsating and throbbing.

"Ride the wave," he said, continuing to massage with his fingers on both hands. "Keep riding, you've got a way to go. Keep going, keep going."

I don't know how many I had or how long the explosive orgasms lasted. The sensitivity finally lessened, and coming down I felt not only satisfied but also peaceful and calm. Frankly, considering this experience, I don't know if I'd *ever* had a real orgasm. Certainly nothing like this.

AFTER CHANGING MY CLOTHES, I met Javier out at

the desk area. For some strange reason I wasn't embarrassed that his hands had been all in and over my naked body, and I thanked him for the life-changing experience.

"Can you see now what I am doing? Where I am going?"

"It seems to be all about releasing tension."

"Absolutely correct," he responded, looking pleased. "For women to reach their sexual potential, as well as dealing with trauma and personal issues. Women's orgasms are so much more complicated than men's and they can use all the help they can get. You see, it's educational, as well as scientific. In fact, women given an MRI, you know, magnetic resonance imaging, after orgasm show a definite tension release, particularly in the brain. After many workshops, courses and clinics in San Francisco, New York, Los Angeles, England and India, I have received official certification in Sexological Bodywork, learning to increase blood flow and sensitivity to the vaginal area. Also, it's a question of equality. Males can get a fifty-minute massage and have an orgasm in the last ten minutes in most cities today. Believe me, at least ninety percent of *all* men, whether or not they have used the services of a massage parlor with happy endings included, know where they are located close by."

"I like the way you put it all on a therapeutic and scientific basis. It takes the whole subject out of the dark and sits it squarely in the sunshine. But what about you? You're fully dressed, there's no reciprocation, kissing or actual sex allowed, so who takes care of you?"

"Where do you think I was minutes before you came in today?" He blushed. "I like to start my mornings with a clean slate, so to speak."

The phone rang. "I better take this," I said. "So interesting. More info later?"

Javier gave me a thumbs-up and went to get coffee from the coffeemaker in one of the massage rooms.

Clearing my throat, I picked up the phone. "Massage Time, may I help you? You say you want to schedule a session and you have a coupon? Wait! Is this you, Mom?"

Chapter Fourteen

AT TWO O'CLOCK JAVIER LEFT to get some lunch. I tried to speak to him but he pointed at the clock on the sidewall and said he needed one hour, then we'd talk when he returned.

So far all was well on my first day plus his noon appointment floated out of here like a feather caught in a summer breeze, completely satisfied with her massage.

And why not?

I quickly tapped on Leigh's number in my phone.

"Get over here. I don't care if you're working on a real estate deal to buy the Taj Mahal for some Manhattan billionaire. I've got stuff to tell!"

"Give me ten minutes."

SHE MADE IT IN FIVE!

"Ready for the *BIG REVEAL*?"

"Give it to me straight, Suzanne." Leigh's voice collapsed as she bent over with hands on her knees, gasping for breath after running the length of the strip mall and up the circular staircase.

"Javier gives massages and brings women to an

87

orgasm because—wait for it—he's clinically trained and is certified in the female climax and wants to help women unlock their full sexual potential."

Silence.

"That's it? No secret dirty old man desires, no grabbing his cock and masturbating under the massage table, no deep French kissing while aiming his dick at his client's cunt?"

"Nope, nope, and nope, and Javier's only twenty-eight. Not a dirty old man yet."

"Holy shit! So that's it. He wants to give us pleasure. What are the odds?"

"Now I've been trying to figure out how I can buy Massage Time and harness this Force of Nature for myself and, of course, you," I said, laughing. "Except I only have savings of a hundred and forty-six dollars."

Leigh frowned. "My bank account is a bit underfunded, too. Well, let me go back to the office and find out what this place rents or sells for."

"I was just kidding, Leigh. I don't want the whole building. I just want Javier and his golden hands—and fingers."

"Hey, maybe your organized and list-making mother might want to invest in a worthy cause."

"Yikes! My mother! That reminds me I've got to tell Javier she's coming over for a massage tomorrow. He *must* tone down his approach."

"So your mother isn't entitled to discover the health benefits of an orgasm and to reach her full sexual potential?"

"I guess so but I don't want to know anything about it. She's my mother, for God's sake."

"Well, if you notice, Javier is not a massage and

tell type of person. He never said what he did with you and never told you what he did with me."

"Kinda like what we learned in Al-Anon about anonymity."

"Yes, but I hope you don't mind because I *did* tell Sally, you know the waitress at Pam's Place, to try Javier because his massage is somewhat arousing."

"Arousing? LOL a freakin' understatement."

I WAS ON THE LOOKOUT FOR JAVIER and rushed to him as he came back through the glass doors. "Listen, we've got to talk. There's a situation—"

"Nothing we can't handle, Suzanne."

"Not 'we,' it's me."

"Okay, what's the problem?"

"My mother's coming for a massage tomorrow."

"Ah, I see. What I can say is that I will treat her just like anyone else. Is that what you wanted to hear?"

"No. She's my *mother*, Javier."

"I understand. Really I do. I will give your mother the massage she wants and came for. You and I have worked together so you know I take my cue from the person on the table. Actually, some people will come here just wanting a plain massage, and I will happily honor that request. Are you okay with what I'm saying?"

"Yes. And I don't want to know *any* details."

"I *never* give any. To anyone. Ever."

WHEN I GOT HOME MOM was taking her dinner out of the oven. I looked at the cooking sheet with all kinds of cut up roasted vegetables on it covered with mozzarella cheese. "This looks good, Mom. Got any extra?"

"Absolutely. Put another setting on the patio table and I'll bring it right out. By the way, how was your first day? I can't wait for my massage tomorrow."

"All good, Mom," I said, then changed the subject. "Now that you spooned the veggies onto the beautiful blue and white china platter, it looks even better," I remarked as she put the big dish down on the colorful paisley placemat of blues, beiges and rusts.

"Daddy bought that for me on our first Thanksgiving. He said every woman needs a big turkey platter to use for Thanksgiving dinner. I remember rolling my eyes, knowing he meant the holiday was always going to be at our house."

"And we *did* have crowds, didn't we, Mom?"

"That's because Daddy invited anyone who looked even slightly lonely. Neighbors, friends, relatives, business associates, people he met at the supermarket and on and on." She stopped mid-thought. "Actually, that's one of the main reasons why he drank so much. He was hypersensitive about the world's pain. He couldn't bear to see people's sad eyes or hear their sad stories."

"Were you upset when we had so many for Thanksgiving dinner?"

"No, I just bought more turkeys—and more turkey platters."

"Just talking about Dad makes me miss him. I loved him so much."

"I know you did. And he loved you, more than anyone or anything."

"Sometimes I think when that terrible train ended

90

his life in a brief second, it ended part of mine, too. He'll never kiss me again, never put his arm around my shoulder, I'll never hear him whisper his sound advice—"

We both laughed a little uneasily and together uttered the four words that finished the familiar sentence—"that usually contradicted Mom's."

"Suzanne, it's so good when we remember Daddy together, and I think tonight is the perfect time I shared something with you."

I didn't like the sound of that.

"As you know I was Dad's legal wife, responsible for his debts and executor of his will."

"Oh, Mom," I gave her hands a light squeeze. "Do you need some money? I'm a working girl now."

She shook her head. "No, I'm financially set. But you know how Daddy, on his sober days, always said it was good to have some money in the bank *in case of emergencies?*"

"Oh yes, I remember, Mom. He left you some then?"

"Well, he did, and there's some for *you*, too."

"Me?"

"Thank goodness you are divorcing Frank. God forbid if he knew about the money; that alcoholic man would go through it in no time. I made a decision to seal the account until you were thirty or divorced Frank, whichever came first. Some of the money came from Dad's investments after his lucrative career on Wall Street, and the rest from the payout provided by the railroad's insurance company when their train hit Dad's car."

I sucked in a breath and listened.

"All together it comes to approximately three million dollars."

"Whaaat?" I couldn't talk or move. I just sat there with my forehead buried in my hands. Tears spilled down through my fingers landing on my knees as I processed everything I heard.

No, no, not blood money from Dad's death.

"You can see my lawyers when it's convenient for you. They will give you options for investing or saving your money. But it is of utmost importance that your financial interests are protected."

Mom could see I was obviously in a jumbled state, unable to think intelligently.

"Suzanne, sweetheart, Daddy would want you to have it—*in case of emergencies.*"

I laughed through my tears, and we hugged knowing that was exactly what Dad would have said and wanted.

THE MOMENT WE STARTED to clear the table and clean up, Buddy wanted to play Toss the Slobbery Tennis Ball.

"No fetch tonight, Bud. I've got to go to work in the morning."

Poor little thing, his ears went down and his eyes got that wistful look.

"All right, three tosses. That's it," I said, thinking we could both use a diversion. "One." I called out and threw the ball.

In no time Buddy retrieved it.

"Two." I threw it even further in the yard, and he returned it.

"Three."

I stepped behind me to wing it higher this time and fell backward over a big branch, landing on my butt—and came face to face with the dragonfly. Again, it darted and dove, doing multiple loop-de-loops and always stopping to hover in front of my eyes.

"Yes, yes, I'll remember to welcome changes, live in this day only and investigate before making any decisions. But listen, your life span is, uh, short. You can't waste another day, hour or minute on *me*. Go find a mate and lay your eggs. Tick, tock. Tick, tock."

It reversed and flew away just as Buddy brought me the ball.

Getting to my feet, I brushed the grass and leaves off the back of my dress. I rounded up Buddy and his bag of tennis balls and took a few more dishes into the kitchen.

"Mom, guess who I met out on the lawn? The Dragonfly!"

"That's great. By the way, I did some more reading and found out it's the world's fastest flying insect, propelling itself at speeds of nineteen to thirty-eight miles per hour. Supposedly, the dragonfly symbolizes how swiftly we can come to new insights and conclusions if we are open to them. So keep watch for those opportunities, Suzanne. Oh, there's the knock on the front door. It's Linda, you know, Mrs. Tracy, our neighbor down the street. When she heard you were home, she baked us a triple-berry pie with blueberries, raspberries and gooseberries. She grew all the berries in her own garden. And she always thought you were such a cutie."

"Sounds yummy," I called out to Mom.

First, three million dollars, now a triple-berry pie!

I took the chain off, then proceeded to undo the

lock, not before I heard a loud voice.

"Open. The Fucking. Door."

Oh. Damn. Jerry.

"You can't come in," I yelled through the open crack but then remembered what the dragonfly said about welcoming transformation and change, "unless you pay a toll."

"Okaaay," he shouted, obviously exasperated. "What's the toll, Suz?"

"A kiss."

Chapter Fifteen ✕

SLAMMING THE DOOR OPEN, Jerry pulled me against his hard body with one hand and cupped my chin upwards with the other. His gaze fell to my mouth. He lowered his head, and his eyes were closed as his lips lightly touched mine.

More of that, please.

Screwing up my courage, I reached up and threaded my hands through his thick, chestnut-brown hair and around his neck. Getting the picture from my move, he opened his steel blue eyes, pulled his hands tighter around my waist and pushed me against the wall as I gripped his shoulders. My pulse raced, and I could hardly catch a breath but there was no stopping now—for either of us. Leaning my upper body back, I allowed my lower body to come forward and grind into his growing erection. Bending down, his lips met mine with increased intensity. The harder the pressure, the more we opened our mouths to feel each other's tongues explore and devour. We were in sync. This was it. This was the way I always wanted to be kissed—and never was.

I broke away first, sensing something behind me. It was Mrs. Tracy holding the pie.

"Sorry, I'll just take this into the kitchen," she said rushing by us.

"Oh my God," we heard her say to my mother, "That was better than any Hollywood movie kiss I've ever seen."

"I've thought about us for a long time," Jerry whispered as our bodies stayed close together. "It's our time now, Suz. Just you and me. Finally."

"Hold it, Jerry." I put my hand up in front of his ruggedly handsome face. "I've got a lot of questions, I'm sure you have a few. We *need* to talk. But I've got to get up early for my new job.

"New job. Where?"

"I'm the receptionist at Massage Time—you know, in Pleasant Hill. The same strip mall as Chesterton Realty."

"Okay. Let's meet at that little deli there tomorrow night after you finish work."

Not good. All I could think of was Sally coming up to our table, peppering me with questions about Massage Time. "Oh, you mean Pam's Place? Nah, not always thrilled with the food."

"Well then, why don't we meet at the Courtside Diner on the other side of Pleasant Hill?"

"Yes. I'll text you when I leave work."

Jerry turned; his hand was on the doorknob when something shot out from the kitchen and landed at his feet. "Buddy!" he yelled and bent down to give the dog that remembered him a belly rub. "I love this dog," he said, looking a bit teary-eyed as Buddy jumped up to give him slurpy-doggie kisses on the chin. "I'll see you soon, Budster."

Before shutting the door, Jerry pointed to Buddy

and said, "Man's best friend. How about us?"

"Okay. Friends it is, then," I called out as he walked to his car.

"Oh, no bay-bee! Not after *that* kiss," he yelled back, a trace of male laughter in his voice lingered in the air.

※

"THANKS, MOM, BUT NO PIE for me now. Gotta get to bed. Yes, Jerry was here, and we're going to meet for dinner tomorrow after work. Goodnight. I love you," I said as I ran upstairs, reluctantly adding, "See you tomorrow at Massage Time."

"Goodnight, sweetie. Love you, too."

Tonight I wanted to wear one of Daddy's t-shirts, to draw in his scent as the dad I loved and thank him for the money for emergencies, and perhaps going back to school. True, the money made me feel a little more relaxed about my future, even though I was enjoying my new job. In the few short days I'd been at Massage Time, I felt like less of a loser because I had a purpose there. I wanted to support Javier in his idea of a regulated and safe service for women to find their sexual potential.

No vibrator tonight. Instead, I just wanted to drift off to sleep thinking about Jerry. I knew I didn't want to get myself into another bad relationship. But. Oh. My. God. That. Kiss. An earthquake magnitude of 10 on the Richter scale!

※

"HI, LEIGH," I SAID THE NEXT MORNING as she came through the glass doors. "You're first on the list for a massage today. Room One."

97

"First. That's good so Javier won't be all worn out. I really need his superhuman powers today. My ex is challenging the divorce."

"I'm so sorry, Leigh. Hey, the Al-Anon meeting is tomorrow night at seven o'clock. Want to grab some coffee and talk afterward?"

"Perfect," she said as I showed her to Room One.

Javier followed, went in and shut the door. He came out a minute later to let her undress.

"I talked to the owner," his voice lowered as he spoke to me. "I told her we needed to hire another massage therapist. She said okay but she's now in the middle of negotiating the sale of this place and said it would be up to the new owner." He turned back to Room One. "Better get started with Ms. Chesterton. We'll talk later."

I looked at the clock when Leigh finished. She was only in there forty-five minutes but had booked a ninety-minute massage.

Giddy with pleasure, she almost staggered out of Room One. "Well, I was halfway there when I walked in today, just knowing what was to come. To come," she laughed, "Get it? To come."

"I get it. And I'm so glad. You needed something to relax. Something better than, uh, let's say, chamomile tea."

"Chamomile tea. Pfffttt!" she said with a short backhanded wave as she made her exit out the glass doors. "See you tomorrow night after the meeting."

I RESOLVED TO STRAIGHTEN OUT the energy flow in Massage Time. A little Feng Shui, I told Javier, to create some harmony and balance and make it an inviting environment. I did it in the f-ing trailer with Frank so we could at least get passed each other on the way to the bathroom.

As I was moving furniture around, Sally came in. Her nerves were visibly jangled so I pushed two chairs together for a private chat. "Nervous, Sally?"

"So nervous. I was going to call and cancel but my husband said I looked fat and ugly in my denim shorts."

"Yikes! What did you say?"

"So I got some balls and came out with my old standby. 'Have you looked at yourself in your uniform lately? Your stomach is at least ten inches out beyond your feet.'"

"Uniform?" I swallowed hard, hoping the guy worked at Wendy's.

"Yes, Don's the County Sheriff."

"Did you tell him where you were going and for what?"

"Are you kidding? Silent revenge is the best revenge. If I get turned on today, I will go to bed a happy woman."

"Remember, Sally, what happens at Massage Time stays at Massage Time."

"You got it, girl. I'm not messing this up," she said as Javier came and took her into Room Three.

TWO HOURS LATER SALLY EMERGED. She looked spent and dazed with messy bed hair. "Am I lucky or what?" she said softly. "The restaurant I own is only five stores away from this place. Put me in for next

Friday at two."

She tried to push open the glass doors to leave but had no arm strength. I ran and gave her some help. As I held the door for Sally, my mother came in.

"Oh my, the furniture has been all moved around."

"Do you like it, Mom?" I questioned. "There's more room now and in the corner coffee, tea and bottled water available for clients and staff."

"Did you do all this yourself, Sweetie?"

"I couldn't stand it anymore. I needed a project."

"How do you do, Mrs. Quinlan. I'm Javier, your massage therapist," he announced, coming from the back and extending his hand.

"So good to meet you, Javier."

"Let me show you to Room Two, and we'll discuss your preferences before we begin."

And that was that.

PROMPTLY AT SIX O'CLOCK Mom finished her massage and came back into the lobby. She looked flushed but her smile was serene. "That was the best Swedish massage I've ever had. So relaxing, so tension releasing. That Javier. He's something else."

"Yes, he certainly is."

"Next time he feels I could handle a bit more pressure and will do some deep tissue massage. When he talks about what he's doing while he's working on me, I feel like I'm going to massage school."

Knowing Mom, she'll try for an A+.

"So glad you liked it. Maybe I'll see you later at home after I meet Jerry for dinner. But Mom, don't wait up."

CHANGING INTO MY TWO-PIECE floral jumpsuit I'd brought with me to work, I tied the tails of the sleeveless top into a knot above my waist. I wanted sexy. With my black patent high slip-on wedges, I was ready for Jerry and whatever happened.

I drove into the empty rear lot of the Courtside Diner and parked near the back door in case I needed a quick getaway. As the time got nearer to go inside, I began to regret my decision to see Jerry. But there was no choice but to finish what I started. Could an unforgettable kiss turn friends into lovers or lovers into friends? I was game to find out.

Getting out of my van, the stars appeared extremely bright. There was a full moon, too. Laughing to myself, I remembered Mom always said, "That's when the werewolves come out." I entered the diner looking for Jerry.

A waitress pointed to a booth in the back corner and whispered, "He's really good- looking."

I grinned and nodded in the affirmative.

I searched my brain for an opener. "Are you the werewolf I was supposed to meet?"

He stared at me then burst out laughing.

"You saw that full moon, too? Better guard your neck, I'm after blood."

"Maybe *I'm* the werewolf." I put up my hands imitating claws.

"You can suck my neck anytime, Suz."

"Okay, enough with the vampire stuff. Let's order, I'm starving."

"I'm glad to see you can still have fun and make

jokes."

"I do love to be silly from time to time."

I ordered a veggie omelet. He got a club sandwich. I ate but hardly tasted mine because I was determined to ask direct questions and really listen to his answers.

"So, Jerry, talk to me."

"Ask me whatever. I promise to answer honestly. But I'm happy to just sit here and look at you in that sexy outfit."

"That's very nice to hear but my father was an alcoholic, Frank was an alcoholic, so why would I be interested in another alcoholic?"

"Whoa! I'm not an alcoholic. What gave you that impression?"

"You own a bar. I just assumed you drank a lot."

"You never saw me drink at Dr. Unk's. And when you own a bar, it's smart to stay sober. Lately, actually, since you left, I realized I didn't want to spend all my nights in a bar."

I looked up and saw him pause. His deep blue eyes were looking me over, taking me in.

Sexual ooze. That's what he had, sexual ooze.

"I don't get it, Jerry. You were so nice when I first came to Dr. Unk's, and then you went underground."

"I know and I'm sorry. I guess I was still hurt that you ran off and married someone else. I had to make a decision to cut you out of my life because I was determined to spend my time making the bar a big success and because I didn't want to be hurt again. It was very difficult to see you waitressing in that sexy, skimpy outfit every day. I turned away from you a lot so you wouldn't see I was getting a hard-on. I hope you can understand."

"Did your sadness over me drive you to screw with lots of women?"

"Not lots, a few. But they didn't count. I wasn't into any of those relationships. I really wanted you."

Unsure of what to say, I was overwhelmed by his humility and, hopefully, his honesty. He really had a heart. And he sure was handsome.

We talked until eleven when I yawned.

"Suz, it's really late and you have to get up early for work. I have one more thing to say, it's a surprise, and I'll tell you outside. I'll ask you *my* questions about *your* life decisions another time."

"You're right. Thank you for dinner. Yes, we'll do it again."

"OH MY GOD," I SAID AS JERRY walked me to my van. "There was no one else in this parking lot when I came in. Now it's swarming with cars, and the diner's empty. Why are all these cars here?"

Jerry looked puzzled for a minute, then threw his head back and roared with laughter.

"What, what? I want in on the joke."

"You can't be in on the joke. It's for men only. See that little door at the back of the diner? That leads to a Rub &Tug place. An underground massage parlor where you can get a happy ending."

"How do you know that?"

"When I was a senior in high school I went with the guys. I was pretty drunk at the time."

"You never told me about it. Of more importance, were the girls pretty?"

"They were Russian girls, and yeah, they were

pretty. Not as pretty as you, of course. At another time there's a few funny stories about that night. But I want to tell you my surprise before we split."

Hard as it was to rip my head away from thoughts of the combination Courtside Diner/massage parlor, I said, "Oh yes, the surprise. Tell me, please."

"Over the years I've socked away some money. Dr. Unk's was a gold mine. But now I want out of the bar business and to move back to this area so today I went to a realtor to see what was available. Bottom line: I'm in negotiations to buy Massage Time."

Chapter Sixteen ✕

"NO, NO, NO. ABSOLUTELY NOT! You *can't* buy Massage Time!"

"Why not, for God's sake? I thought you'd be happy."

"Well, because, because *I'm* buying it."

"Wait a minute." Jerry looked confused. "The realtor didn't say there were any other offers on it."

"What agency did you go to?"

"The Chesterton agency and spoke to Rose."

"Rose! She doesn't know jack shit, er, anything." I silently but quickly chastised myself for cursing—something I perfected living with Frank. And something I was now trying to tone down.

"Suz, Rose Chesterton is the *owner* of the Chesterton agency."

My face felt flushed, and I was beginning to sweat. "Hold on, let me make a call."

At the same time Jerry's phone went off. "Really? Your ring tone is still the movie theme from The Pink Panther?"

"Hello, Rose." Jerry turned his back to me and lowered his voice. "Yes. This is Jerry Spinella. What? There *was* another offer on Massage Time? But I should hold tight. When will you get back to me? Okay, yes tomorrow's fine."

Leigh sank Jerry's deal. Thank. You. God.

"I'm so sorry, Suz, I had no idea you were interested in buying Massage Time. I was looking for something I could own that I didn't have to live in 24/7. And something that was health-oriented with a relaxing atmosphere and didn't serve booze. But really I did it for you."

"Well, thank you, Jerry. Let's see what happens. I bet it was my friend Leigh, Rose's niece, who put in a bid."

"That's okay. It was a shot in the dark. I'm not upset. Are you?"

"Not really. I'm very fond of Leigh."

"Man, you were really worked up at first, though."

"True but a nice kiss would put me at ease."

I saw the smile in his eyes as Jerry pulled me into his arms. I inhaled his manly scent and exhaled a sigh of contentment. When I tightened my arms around his torso, he bent down and nuzzled my neck.

"Oh God, I forgot you were the world's best neck nuzzler."

An intense feeling of electricity went from my neck downward. I grabbed Jerry's hand and pulled him toward my van just as horns in the parking lot blared, car lights blinked on and off and men shouted out their windows.

"Get a room."

"Show us her tits."

"Do her right here."

"What the fuck are you waiting for?"

"Man up!"

Jerry broke away, then shoved me into my van. "Get going. These horny guys are high on testosterone or frustrated from no testosterone and are waiting for their turn inside. I'll call you tomorrow, and we can sort it all out."

I started the engine but he signaled to me to lower the window, I guess for one last word.

"Never forget, Suz. Men can be nice on the surface but inside all men are pigs."

"Does that include you?"

"*All* men are pigs."

"MOM, LONG DAY. I'M GOING right to bed."

Buddy jumped down from the couch with Mom and looked up at me. I picked him up and gave him kisses on his sweet head and smooth ears.

"Did you have a nice time with Jerry?"

"Very nice and yes, I'll be seeing him again."

"I have a surprise for you. Do you want to hear it now or tomorrow morning?"

I'm beginning to hate surprises.

Jokingly, I said, "You didn't put in an offer on Massage Time, did you?"

Mom took in a sharp breath, "I did."

I was so tired I couldn't rally quick enough to protest. "That's really nice but can we discuss it in the morning?"

"Yes, certainly. Goodnight. Love you."

"Love you, too, Mom."

Trudging upstairs, I barely got undressed before I crashed into bed and let sleep drown out all the confusion doing laps in the swimming pool of my mind.

FUCKING ALARM! I SMACKED the snooze button and rolled over. Slowly, I stretched and stretched again before real life hit me. I threw off the covers and bolted out of bed. Feet on the floor and into the shower, letting the spray wash away the fogginess and feelings of what? Sadness, powerlessness, anger? As I was mentally psyching myself up into a better frame of mind, a jolt of clarity slammed into me like a boxer's uppercut to the jaw.

Leigh. She was the solution!

Drying off, I heard my phone buzz. Grabbing it, I looked at the screen. Leigh texted: *Put in offer on Massage Time. Got in at end of line. We need to talk. Call me on your way to work.*

Ah, yes, bright minds think alike.

"Suzanne," Mom yelled up from the kitchen. "Want a green smoothie? I've got extra."

"Great—I'm on the way down."

"Well, you look rested. Had a good sleep?"

Dressed in a short jeans skirt, red sleeveless t-shirt and sneakers I felt geared up to kick ass and ready to deal. "Enough sleep, thanks. So, tell me, Mom, you put in a bid on Massage Time?"

"I did it for you, sweetheart. Before some stranger bought it."

Why do people do things "for me" without asking me?

I took a long swallow of the smoothie. "I think my friend Leigh put a bid on it, too."

"Is that okay with you?" Mom asked.

"Yes. It's perfect."

I TAPPED ON LEIGH'S NUMBER as I got into my van and put the phone on speaker. Immediately, I heard her voice.

"Suzanne, don't you think this whole thing is a riot? A real circus of bidding wars."

"But nobody knows what they're actually buying except you—that is, if Javier is going to stay as the number one massage therapist. Now here's the good news: Both my Mom and Jerry are willing to back out so that leaves you—*unless* you want to go in partnership with me."

"Whoa! That would be the best. But I thought you didn't have any money."

"There's been a change on that score. Details later but know whatever I need to pony up is okay. Make the deal, then call me back. My gut tells me we'll be great partners."

"Your gut and my gut, too!" Excitement and joy bubbled over in her voice.

"So, Leigh, what's our next step?"

"Let me get all the paperwork ready in the office, then I'll see you at the meeting and for coffee afterward. We'll go from there."

"Looking forward to it, Leigh."

After hanging up, I smiled to myself and sat back as I drove.

No worries. We got this.

I BURST THROUGH THE GLASS doors and couldn't wait to see Javier. "Oh there you are," I said as I saw him at the coffeemaker. "You're not going to believe this. My friend Leigh and I are going in as partners in buying Massage Time. You are going to have your dream clinic where women, *all* women, can experience and be taught the techniques of sexual pleasure with a well-trained massage therapist. What do you think?"

"I think my prayers have been answered," he said, his smile and surprise obviously genuine. "And the prayers of many women who need healing from vaginal trauma, surgery, a painful Caesarian or intimacy issues have been answered, too. What can I do? How can I help?"

"Until all the paperwork is completed, you can begin to think of a few other men or women who do your kind of, uh, therapeutic massages."

"Well, the last place I worked was in New York City. I got sick of the city life and wanted to see trees, water and sky. I do know of a few others who felt the same way so when you're ready I'm sure they'd be willing to come for an interview and demonstration of their skills."

"Excellent, Javier. I'm meeting with Leigh tonight to finalize everything, and after that the three of us will get together. You will be our guide."

"And you, our fearless leader."

"Well, maybe your accidental leader. I'm sure Leigh will want to take over interviewing and auditioning any future employees." I smirked and managed an eye roll.

Javier's serious face was set with quiet assurance. "Sounds like a plan."

I was glad he ignored my not-so-nice tongue in cheek comment about Leigh. Living with a jerk-off drunk like Frank for so many years, I became snide, sarcastic, cynical and at times downright unkind. The three lines my mother taught me got lost in that trailer in South Jersey:

Does it need to be said?

Does it need to be said by me?

Does it need to be said by me now?

THE AL-ANON MEETING STARTED promptly at seven p.m. Leigh flew in breathless several minutes later and sat beside me in the seat I saved. When her breathing settled down, I gave her hand a gentle squeeze. She opened her briefcase and pointed to papers that showed many empty lines that looked ready for signatures. I gave her a big smile, and we both turned our faces toward the leader who announced the topic for tonight's meeting was *ACCEPTANCE*.

A woman, Mia, put her hand up. She led her share with the fact she was one of fraternal twins. Her story was much the same as it was at last week's meeting. Mia and Max, Max and Mia, Mia and Max. *Yawn!* Normal kids argue and fight but not Mia and her brother, Max. Seemed they had an ideal relationship, or so she said, until Mia married David, a handsome local cop and an alcoholic. That's when her story took a detour from last week. I leaned forward in my seat.

She said she just found out that David and his cop buddies had been getting drunk on weekends and going to a massage parlor to get a happy ending. The room sucked in a collective gasp. She had assumed those evenings were her husband's poker nights. Her

111

question was: Should she *accept* David's behavior? And how does she cope with the feelings of anger, betrayal and fear? She told her brother, Max, who encouraged her to leave David and come live with him. Since cross talk was discouraged during the meeting, no one could answer or comment on Mia's question directly, but others shared about how they came to accept things in their own lives while living with an alcoholic. One man said how important it was that he remember an old AA saying about the alcoholic's behaviors and drinking:

> I couldn't stop it.
> I can't cure it.
> I didn't cause it.

Another person quoted the part of the Serenity Prayer that states to "accept the things I cannot change, the courage to change the things I can."

When the meeting was over, Leigh and I raced to our cars and drove to the nearby Courtside Diner.

"Make sure you park in front. I'll tell you why later," I said.

Leigh had all the paperwork ready for me to sign. Mom had transferred money into my account so there was no problem writing a check for my half. As I did I said a silent thank you to my dad.

"I let Javier know we are partners and we want him to fashion Massage Time into his dream clinic for all women. He's very serious about this, and I agree with him."

"I'm with you all the way, Suzanne, but is it legal?"

"Technically, it's legal."

"Technically. What does that mean?"

"Well, it's massage. That's the legal part. Currently, the other therapeutic services are illegal but it's a big injustice and I'll tell you why."

At that point I filled her in about the backdoor business behind the building we were sitting in the Courtside Diner. Her mouth dropped open.

"If there are Russian girls for men, why not Javier for women? And hey, not to break meeting anonymity, but what about the policeman husband and his buddies being serviced? Bet that happened right here in a room below us."

"Just think," Leigh said, a bemused smile on her lips, "the Courtside Diner is a one-stop shop. You can go out for the evening and eat your meat, then afterward beat your meat—all in the same location."

Chapter Seventeen ✈

"DON'T WRITERS SAY 'write what you know'? Well, then you can do this, Suzanne. You know the massage therapist. You know his intent. You know the results. You're smart, and we need some good PR in *The Pleasant Hill Post* to get us going as a new kind of spa."

"Thanks, Leigh. I appreciate your confidence. I'm going to try my best. And I will include being an owner and a customer, too." I was surprised to hear Javier's words echoed my own thoughts. "At this time I would like to insert one caveat before writing a press release."

"Uh oh, what is it?" Leigh's color momentarily drained from her face as Javier joined the conversation. "Give it to us straight."

"I would like to change the name from Massage Time to Dragonfly, then written underneath: A Spa for Her."

"Oh, yes, like the wallpaper downstairs."

"Exactly, Leigh. I've done some reading about the dragonfly. It goes through an unbelievable metamorphosis during years under water to finally emerge as a beautiful and determined four-winged insect. It's a global symbol of transformation, informed decision-making and living in the present."

Javier's smile broadened in approval. "Just what we hope happens to a woman as she matures. Oh and, hopefully, to men, too."

Without hesitation Leigh broke in. "All in favor of the name change from Massage Time to Dragonfly—A Spa for Her, raise your hands."

All three hands shot up at once, and we spent a few joyous moments high-fiving each other.

My phone vibrated. A text from Jerry asking when he could see me. I knew he and I had more things that needed to be said and more problems we wanted to be solved. But for now I just looked forward to folding into his broad chest and being hugged tight.

I texted: *My house tonight 7 pm. Mom has a meeting. I'll cook or you bring Chinese food.*

Jerry's return text: *Chinese. CU 7. XO, J.*

Maybe I was like the dragonfly. What I thought was a losing hand—seven years submerged with Frank in a trailer—now proved to be an epic journey to escape that dormancy and begin to emerge renewed. Or perhaps the dragonfly's magic had orchestrated it all. Either way there weren't any lingering shadows, only a bottomless feeling of right time, right place, right guy.

Before I left for home, Javier said he had received a return call from his friend Steve, who was interested in the position as a second masseuse. Steve's day off was tomorrow so he could get here by two o'clock.

Leigh and I said we could be present at that time for his interview, which was welcome news because appointments were coming in quickly and Javier was working overtime. He said I was never to turn anyone down. And I never did.

JERRY ARRIVED PROMPTLY at seven o'clock with two big brown bags of little white boxes: steaming Moo Shu Shrimp and Vegetables, General Tso's chicken, sesame beef, egg rolls, scallion pancakes, barbecued spare ribs, vegetable fried rice and fortune cookies.

"Whoa, who's going to eat all that?" I said when I opened the door.

He put the bags down, closed the door and leaned against the back of it with his arms and ankles crossed as his eyes took a slow journey from my sandals up to my face. "You are so sexy, Suz. I'm tired of waiting. I want you now. Don't you want me?"

"But we really don't know each other—yet. It's been seven years," I said, fighting his overpowering sexual ooze.

Jerry's body was perfect in tight-fitting jeans and a navy blue polo shirt. No words were said, and no objections from me as he took one foot and pushed off a flip-flop, then did the same with the other. Reaching up with both hands, he pulled his shirt off over his head. The tanned six-pack abs he had in high school were now more defined from all the hard work he did at the bar. His biceps bulged from lifting and bringing in all the liquor and food deliveries from suppliers, carrying it all down to the cellar, then back up when it was needed.

The anticipation of what was to come filled me with excitement and dread. "I'm still a little mad at you, and we need to talk."

"How about we talk after?" Jerry reached for me and eased me into his arms.

I melted into his chest and inhaled his familiar and arousing male scent. I wanted to stop going further but my defenses were weak. I was powerless to resist his eagerness. It excited me.

"After what?" I choked out.

"After we make love or after we fuck. You pick."

"I pick love but I need a little more foreplay."

For me talking is *foreplay.*

Gathering up all my willpower, I blurted out, "First, tell me why you let abusive sex go on upstairs over the bar?"

"Okay, we'll double up. Love and foreplay together."

Not to be deterred, Jerry nibbled down my neck. "God, I can't keep my hands off you, Suz. To be honest, I had no idea what was going on in those upstairs rooms." His little heated kisses at the base of my neck sent tingles through my body. "I let the girls decide for themselves. They did what they did for the money, and they earned it all. I asked for nothing," he said, licking my chest down to the center of my cleavage. "If they had a complaint, they went to Julia."

"That's so creepy, Jerry. Didn't you begin to hate yourself?" A lurch of urgency traveled through me as he pushed my tank top and my bra strap down.

"That's one of the reasons I wanted out of there. When you left I realized there was more to life than giving customers all the booze and sex they wanted."

Couldn't help it. I was squirming and writhing as he pulled one breast free and licked and nuzzled the top and all around it.

"You're killing me, Suz, let's get to the love part," his words punctuated with passionate groans.

"Didn't you feel bad leaving all the people there who depended on you?" I gasped, then moaned as he took my nipple between his teeth and sucked it as he put his hand in my bra and stroked and pulled out my other breast.

"I found people who wanted to buy the bar. The others can decide if they want to stay."

Moving his hand down, he unbuttoned and unzipped my denim shorts. I wriggled as his fingers made their way to the top of my moist clit. And then he stopped.

"Seriously, haven't I answered all of these same questions to your satisfaction? And think back. Aren't you are the one who left me? Can't we say we're even? Can't you meet me halfway? How about any of the following: A do-over? A reset? A second chance?"

As Jerry was beginning to withdraw his fingers from my shorts, I firmly placed my hand down over his.

"Oh, so you *do* want me to continue?"

I nodded. "Don't stop, please. Enough talking. Let's make love."

I touched my lips to his. He returned the kiss with increased intensity and probing with his tongue. My eyes glazed, and I gave in freely to the passion of his kiss and let my tongue search his mouth and lips. The fire was hot and mutual—but what were those noises?

Lots of noises. A scritching and scratching. A licking and slurping. The strong aroma of soy sauce and ginger permeated the air. We turned our heads to see Buddy pulling boxes of Chinese food out of one of the large brown bags on the floor and chowing down.

"Quick," I jumped up. "Don't let him have any spare ribs. No bones for dogs. He'll choke."

"I give up," Jerry said as we cleaned up the mess on the floor. "Next, your mother will come home or some neighbor lady will deliver another pie or aliens will have landed."

"Tell you what," I said, standing on tiptoes with my arms around his neck. "Let's go away somewhere together. Alone."

"Great. When?"

"Next weekend. Sunday and Monday. I get Sunday off, and Leigh can probably cover Monday for me. I do need to tell you I have an IUD because I didn't want to chance having babies with my asshole husband, but we should both get tested. An STD panel and HIV antibody test. I'm going to the Emergency Medical Care office next to the realty office. They'll do it in a few days there. I checked."

"Yes, I'm familiar with that. Julia had the girls at the bar tested regularly. So then we'll be good to go," his look boyishly hopeful. "You're telling me this will be a fresh start for us. Right?"

"I'll get back to you on that," I said, stifling a grin as I picked up and opened the one still sealed fortune cookie. "Listen to this: 'Be aware, something you have kept hidden will appear. Then suddenly disappear.'"

"Well, while I'm waiting for your answer to *my* question, you might want to make something that appeared suddenly disappear, like putting your tits back in your bra."

"Oh. Shit. Jerry. Why didn't you say something?"

"Because it was too much fun watching you bounce around with them out."

Chapter Eighteen ⊁

"HOW'S THIS?" I TURNED MY laptop screen in Leigh's direction. While she was reading I got myself some coffee from the office coffeemaker.

"So you're not going to mention anything about being brought to an orgasm during the massage?" Leigh asked as she looked up from my laptop.

"I'm leaving that to Javier to work out on an individualized basis with each client. I'm putting in several euphemisms like 'tension release' and 'special stretching.' I don't think *The Pleasant Hill Post* will publish anything about 'increasing clitoral sensitivity.' But do you like the title of the piece?"

"*Could You Use A Hand or Two?* Love it. Grabs your attention. Speaking of grab, how was your evening with Jerry? Get some?"

"Another thwarted evening. We ended up cleaning Chinese food off the floor. Don't ask. Oh, by the way, can you cover the desk for me next Monday? If Jerry and I are ever going to have real, honest-to-goodness, down and dirty sex, we are going to have to go away."

"So you two never fucked? Even in high school? I don't get that."

"We kissed and petted a lot, and I did blow jobs on him in his truck. But I got involved with Frank early in my senior year after visiting the shore with girlfriends. I was so thrilled by the beach party life. Surfing all day and at night dancing on the sand to blasting music and drinking ourselves into a stupor. After all that, Frank wasn't interested in being thoughtful and considerate. He just took what he wanted. We had sex the first night we met. Let me restate that: We had *unsatisfactory* sex the first night we met. Frank was so drunk that he passed out on the couch. When I checked on him, he was curled up crying and sucking his thumb."

"Why the hell did you marry such a loser guy?"

"He was fatally attractive and had lots of muscles and an auto body fix-it shop. Also I couldn't wait to get out from under my mother's control and my father's drinking. And Jerry was going to Rutgers for four years. I wasn't going to wait around. I wanted out."

Stupid me.

"Weren't you on the way to college, too?"

"I promised my parents after I married Frank I would go to Ocean County Community College and then transfer to a local four-year college. I did get that two-year degree, but then had to work to pay bills. Mostly, Frank's liquor bills."

"Now what about you, Leigh?"

"Listen, you finish that article and send it to *The Post* ASAP. Then how about lunch at Pam's Place and I'll fill you in on my downhill marriage. At two o'clock we'll come back and interview the new massage guy. Woo hoo!"

"Sounds perfect."

"FRED WAS ALWAYS ON THE HUNT," Leigh said, folding and refolding the corners of her restaurant paper placemat. "We'd be out somewhere and talking to each other but really he was looking over my shoulder and beyond me at some other female or females. Also, he'd lie, telling me he was working late, but he'd come home disheveled and smelling like sweaty sex. Yeah, he drank, but his real addiction was women. I ended up in Al-Anon because of my father's alcoholism, but I sure could've used a Sex-Anon meeting."

"I don't know if there is such a thing. I'm sure there is, best to check online. But to solve all our problems there's only *one* answer: More and better research and investigation before decision-making."

We tapped our ice tea glasses together in mutual agreement.

"Ladies, what are we toasting tonight?" Sally came out from the kitchen carrying our Greek salads. She put them down plus a little dish of extra olives in oil.

"Oooh, olives," Leigh and I said, snatching and eating several at a time.

"These are great, Sally." I licked my fingers and went back for more. "Who makes them? You or Pam?"

Sally's smile faded and her normally expressive face changed becoming somber. "There is no Pam. I'm the only owner, and I named the place after my ten-year-old sister who died thirty years ago when she was caught in a strong undertow after a hurricane at the shore."

We both stood and gave Sally hugs while conveying our condolences for the untimely death of her little sister.

"Pammie loved the water and was a good swimmer, but she ran into the ocean late one afternoon with no lifeguards on duty. My mother didn't even know she left the house—the one we rented for the summer right on the beach—until we discovered she was missing. Days later the police found her body washed up on a nearby jetty. We were so grateful when they found our Pammie and stayed afterwards and talked with us. They even came back the next day and the next. Maybe that's why I married my idiot husband because he was a policeman. I guess I was blinded by the uniform—the cop's blues. I thought he'd be understanding and supportive like the policemen who cared for us at the shore."

"Listen, Sally, there's no one left in here. Come sit with us," I said, patting the seat on the chair beside me. "We were just talking about our idiot ex-husbands. Feel free to join in with your own complaints."

"Certainly less complaints after two sessions with Javier. Now I don't even care if Don comes home late or goes to play poker with the guys."

Leigh and I froze and quickly eyed each other.

"Poker, you say, Sally?" I tried to keep my voice neutral. "Does he play cards often?"

"Only on weekends. Why?"

I was momentarily speechless. Leigh leaned in, her eyes wide and took her chance. "Oh, we heard some of the cops were getting massages with happy endings over behind the Courtside Diner on

123

weekends."

"No, they busted that place long ago," Sally said in a casual way. "But who knows? Maybe it started up again. I'll ask Don."

"Oh, no, don't. I, uh, don't want to start any town gossip. Bad for business."

Leigh concurred.

"Oh dear, we have a meeting at two o'clock," I said, looking at my phone. "We better get back."

We waved goodbye to Sally, and each of us gave her another compassionate hug.

On the way out Leigh shook her head. "I hate when bad things happen to such a good person."

"That's for sure but you and I have to talk later. I figured out a plan to learn the real story on the Courtside Diner situation."

"I knew you would."

"JAVIER, YOU TAKE THE LEAD on this interview because you know what you're looking for and you know the questions to ask."

"But speak up, Suzanne. Don't be shy. Ask what's important to you. And you, too, Leigh."

Steve had a lean, sleek physique and was hard-muscled. Both arms had full sleeve tattooing from wrist to shoulder. All the artwork was in black ink, well executed and beautiful. There was a stunning drawing of a German shepherd on one arm; I guessed it was his dog with the name Zeus printed underneath. Interesting designs and line work filled in the rest. Around the back of his neck was a thin line of calligraphy: "This above all: To thine own self be true." I remembered it was from Shakespeare's *Hamlet*. Steve's blond hair was in a man bun, and the shadow of a beard contrasted with his baby face.

I whispered to Leigh I wanted to pinch his cheeks. And the ones on his face, too.

My questions centered on his motivation for wanting to massage women. His answers were sensitive, seemed honest and very similar to Javier's reasons plus he, too, was sick of city life. As the interview came to a close, he said the one thing I wanted to hear.

"It's unfair. Men can get happy endings anytime, anywhere. Women should have the same right. There's no reason why not."

"I like the way you think, Steve," I said. "But are you willing to take on any woman as a client who comes through the door, no matter who or what?"

"Absolutely, that's why I'm here, to support any woman who wishes help. I truly believe beauty comes in all sizes, shapes and colors." The warmth of his smile echoed in his voice.

When the questioning ended, Steve said, "Which one of you ladies wants to sample my signature massage?"

Before I was finished processing his words, Leigh's hand shot up like a rocket on steroids.

"Go for it, Leigh" I said, eliminating the part about being our resident guinea pig. "When you're finished, let's talk about our plan."

"I hope I won't be able to talk—at least coherently."

"AS FAR AS I'M CONCERNED, this guy's hired," Leigh said as she staggered out of Room Three. "His style is low-key but extremely caring and really sweet. I'll give you some specifics later."

"Did you tell Javier you liked the massage?"

"Yes, I gave him a thumbs-up."

"Hopefully, Steve can start here soon. I don't know how much notice he has to give to his New York place. But come over to the coffeemaker area. Javier's in with him, probably discussing those details so we can talk about my plan to investigate the Courtside Diner."

"Okay, Suzanne. Don't keep me in suspense. Does it include handguns, backup by Navy SEALs, putting hidden audio and video devices in all of the rooms or sending over Javier and Steve to get hand jobs, then reporting back?"

"Well, you're half right."

"Oooo, Navy SEALs?"

"No Navy SEALs. But it does include hidden devices and two men planted inside their business to get the real scoop."

"So Javier and Steve will go there and maybe even partake in their services?"

"Nope," I said, shaking my head. "The two men going undercover will be you and me."

Chapter Nineteen ✗

I WAS GETTING PISSED. Just thinking about the Courtside Diner, the gender divide and injustice made ending the article for *The Pleasant Hill Post* daunting. There were so many truths I wanted to express and expose but I also wanted to point out that Dragonfly— A Spa for Her had what women wanted and needed. I listed six phrases I wanted to include:

1. You will find a partnership between yourself and your massage therapist.

2. You will have knowledge of a new chapter in the massage story.

3. You will connect with the real you inside.

4. Together we will push your emotional and physical boundaries with the end result of tension release.

5. Don't remain on the outside looking in.

6. You will experience a new energy and finish in a state of grace.

Well, maybe "state of grace" *was* going a bit overboard.

"You're here so early," said Leigh. "How come?"

Groaning, I put my head in my hands, "I can't seem to wrap up this article. There is so much I want to say and can't. Help me, Leigh."

"Listen, in this type of massage biz we have to count on word-of-mouth marketing. Like Sally. She heard about it from us; she didn't read it in a newspaper. Now she's very enthusiastic and can't wait to book a session with Steve. All she needed was our verbal invitation."

"*INVITATION!* That's it! Thanks, Leigh. I can start out by saying, 'I invite you to change your life.' And maybe *The Post* can help make it look like a real engraved invitation."

As the words began to flow, I gathered my thoughts and my courage. That's when the article finished itself. "After doing all the research for this article, maybe I'll write a book about sexual democracy for women. I'll call it *Orgasm Injustice* or, on a more positive note, *Orgasm Justice*. No, better yet, *Orgasm Equality.*"

"Great idea but right now tell me more about us going undercover. Aren't the Russian girls going to get a little suspicious when we undress and they see we have tits instead of dicks?"

"We're not undressing. We will be wearing disguises to look like male teenagers sneaking out late at night hoping to get a hand job. Our purpose will be to take pictures and record anything important on our phones. That way if, and when, the police decide they want to shut *us* down, we can basically say, "Then why are *you* ignoring men getting happy endings behind the Courtside Diner?' At that point we'll hold up our phones and say here's the proof that sexual contact there is ongoing."

"Yes, I get it. It's *evidence!"* Leigh sounded convinced. "So when is 'Dinergate' going into play?"

"That's your name for the plan?"

"Every undercover special ops unit has a code name for a new assignment."

"Okay, how about next Tuesday for Dinergate? There's young men who got drunk and didn't get any over the weekend and middle-aged men who fantasized about coworkers and divorcees and didn't get any either. And, of course, there's the typical married man who thinks he's really single anyway and has convinced himself getting a hand job doesn't count as cheating. All of the above should be fairly horny by Tuesday. So get yourself a baseball cap and a big shirt that won't show your boobs. We actually might want to wrap our chests so we look flat. Wear jeans, not tights and sneakers, and no nail polish, make-up or lipstick. Tell no one, not even Javier."

"But tell me again why you don't have Javier and Steve do this?"

"Because I know what needs to be observed, noted and photographed, and I don't want to take the chance they'll fuck it up."

"Suzanne, that's one hell of a clever plan."

"Thanks. But if anything nasty starts to come our way, just like the Boy Scouts, we are going to BE PREPARED."

FRIDAY CAME AND WENT. Saturday came and went. Sunday came. Today's the day! Jerry and me alone, fucking and fucking and fucking. And maybe some sucking, too. Who am I kidding? There's always licking before sticking.

"Got everything, Suzanne?" Mom yelled up the

stairs. "Jerry's outside in the car."

"I'm coming." I already had a rolling duffle bag down in the hall and was just finishing throwing last minute stuff in a tote.

Mom kissed me goodbye and, with a sort of a secret smile, told me to have a good time. Obviously, she knew what we were up to. "When you come back, I'll share my interesting news."

I stopped, "What news? You know I hate surprises."

"No worries, sweetie," she said, putting her arm around me and giving my shoulder a squeeze. "I met a nice man at my Al-Anon meeting. We've had a few dates."

"That's nice, Mom." But all I could think of was my poor dead dad.

"Oh, here comes Jerry to help with your bags."

Jerry said hello to Mom and stooped to give Buddy a head pet and ear scratch.

"We'll be home late Monday, Mom. Don't wait up."

"I might be out on a date when you get here," she said. "But don't be concerned. I'll be safe. He's a policeman."

✻

"SO, SUZ, WHAT'S YOUR CHOICE?" Jerry said as he started his truck. "Shore or Adirondacks?"

"Huh? Oh, uh, how about the Adirondacks for a change?" My mind was totally clogged with thoughts of Mom's relationship with a local policeman. Was he one of those in on the Courtside Diner activities? Damn, I don't want to ruin my trip with Jerry thinking about it.

"Suz. Are you okay? You don't seem happy."

"Sorry, Jerry. I'm very happy. Really excited. Just distracted by some things at work. But I'm all yours now."

"Good, 'cause we're going all the way past Lake George up to Lake Placid."

"Sounds great. Anywhere as long as I'm with you. So talk to me, let's get to know each other as you drive. Tell me what's going on with your job hunt?"

"I've been doing a lot of thinking about what I really want, what I really believe in. After so many years being around drunks in a bar, I keep coming back to working with people about self-care and helping them reach their fitness goals. I think that's why I considered buying your massage place. So when I was talking to Rose Chesterton, she also showed me a gym in Summit that was for sale. It's in good shape and has room to hang a few rows of heavy bags."

"For boxing, right?"

"Yes, kickboxing, too. I had a mini gym set up in the basement of Dr. Unk's. Just throwing a few combination punches helped me get rid of tension. But the gym in Summit also has state-of-the-art equipment as far as weights go and a few treadmills, ellipticals, exercise bikes and rowing machines. Eventually, I could add classes like yoga, Zumba, Pilates and also personal training."

"You've really thought this through. I like it. I really do. And you could keep up with your own workouts," I said, trailing my finger around his well-muscled bicep. "Hey, you could call it Jerry's Jym. Get it? Gym with a J."

"Maybe. I was thinking Fusion Fitness."

"Oh, better yet. A modern, manly name. But you do know they'll end up calling it Jerry's."

"That's what happened at the bar. Dr. Unk's was too hard to remember, especially when you're loaded."

"But don't exclude the ladies from your gym."

"Never. Maybe you could be an instructor."

"Of what?"

"Blow jobs," he said, pulling the truck into a rest stop and grabbing my hand.

"We've only gone a few miles. Do you want coffee or are you hungry?"

"Suzanne, I can't wait till we get to Lake Placid. I want you. I need you. Now."

"I want you, too. Can you hang on until we drive under those trees?" I said, pointing to the back of the parking lot.

Jerry eased into a space with overhanging branches and cut the engine. "My test results. I'm clear so don't worry," he said, waving a paper.

"Me, too. Want to see?"

"I believe you. Put the paper away."

Fully clothed, he pulled me into his arms. With a shift of my weight I pushed back on my hips to get as close to his chest as possible. Crushing me to him, he pressed his lips on mine and suddenly, I was experiencing the hottest, wildest kiss ever. Explosive currents raced through me as our tongues sought the key to each other's sexual arousal. Finally, the strong hardness of his lips decreased as we both broke for air. He raised his mouth from mine and looked into my eyes.

"I'll never get enough of you. Ever."

132

"You have been *my* addiction all these years," I said, unbuttoning his jeans. "I could only think of you and what we had. I want that again."

"No," he said, pushing my hand away. "As much as I love your blow jobs, I want to do you."

"Me first? In your truck?"

"Uh huh," he uttered as he pulled my tank top over my head and unhooked my bra, letting it fall to my waist. "Oh, gotta have those tits."

Putting my hand to the back of his neck, I brought his mouth close to my breasts. He licked each one, then pushed them together, taking both nipples in his mouth at once, suckling and tonguing them and nipping gently as I felt the fire of stimulation heading downward.

"Oh, God, Jerry. I think I'm coming."

"You can't, I have lots more I want to do to you."

"I…I can't stop. It's been too loooong…" I shuddered and shivered repeatedly, then slumped down putting my head in his lap.

We stayed that way for several minutes until the silence was broken with a faint, small voice.

"Mommy, I go pee pee in the bushes by the big twuck."

Our eyes ballooned, and we sunk down low zipping, straightening and hooking our clothing. Easing up to look out the back window, we saw a little boy scamper to his mother.

"I did it good this time," he said, raising his arms up in the air. "I made it go weally, weally high in the sky."

"Not landing on the truck, I hope," she said, her eyes furtively scanning the area as she grabbed his hand and hurried toward their car.

"ARE WE ALWAYS GOING to be doomed by disruptions?" Jerry's chuckle covered his annoyance.

"I got mine." I grinned.

"Now how do I drive four hours to Lake Placid with a raging hard-on?" Jerry's pleading eyes caused a shiver of wanting him to reactivate my sensitive spots and race through me.

"Well, I could suck you right here before getting on the road or we could go to a nice nearby hotel with a swimming pool and Jacuzzi and just relax and have great sex for two days."

"Hotel. Local. Get your phone out and find one. Fast."

"On it."

"No, I want your cunt on it." His smirk telegraphed his desperation.

"I hate the word cunt."

"Pussy?"

"I hate that, too. Gives cats a bad name."

"Vagina, snatch, crotch, vulva, lady parts, twat, hoo-hah, wet heat."

"Good God, you've been hanging around Julia far too long. Hey, found one," I pointed to my phone screen. "The Willow Hotel in Morristown."

"Let's go, Suz," Jerry gunned the engine. "When we get there you'll begin by putting my dick in your mouth."

"I kinda like wet heat."

"That, too."

Chapter Twenty ✕

"TAKE YOUR CLOTHES OFF."

"All off?" I whirled around, quit unpacking and met his gaze with my own.

Watching me from the hotel bed, he was propped up on pillows, arms folded behind his head.

"Panties first."

Reaching under my skirt, I slowly inched the red lace bikini over my hips and let it fall to the floor. They caught on my bare foot and, with one swift kick into the air, I landed them on his chest.

"Direct hit! Now your top."

I pulled down each shoulder strap but held it over my breasts.

"All off," he said.

I peeled off the black tank and threw it toward his face but he caught it first.

"Now what?"

"Bra."

Unhooking my red lace bra, I slipped my arms out of the straps and twirled it over my head. I aimed for the bed but it ended up on my duffle bag.

"Good. Pack it up and don't wear it again while you're here."

"Finished?"

135

"No way. Skirt."

I unbuttoned and unzipped the short denim skirt, letting it shimmy down my legs and pool around my ankles. Picking the skirt up, I threw it, ringing it around his feet.

"Nice throw. Now come here."

"I'm a shy girl."

"You're also a naked girl, and that's what I want. Now get on the bed and undress *me.*"

On my knees I went for his t-shirt first. Up and over his head.

"Next loafers," I said, turning around and allowing each shoe to drop to the floor.

"Nice ass."

"Still best in the class?" Wiggling my backside, I turned my head around to see his cocky male grin.

"Man, a view that never gets old. Now boxers." As I pulled them down his beautiful stiff erection sprung to life.

"Is it as you remember it?"

"Unfuckingbelievable!"

As I closed my lips around the head, I let the tip of my tongue take in his precum. I gathered my saliva and engulfed his very hard cock quickly, stopping for a second to let the sensation sink in. Then, drawing up slowly, I began pulling in with my lips, almost milking him as I moved forward and back always going farther down with each advancing motion. At the same time, reaching underneath his dick, I cupped his balls, stroking and caressing them while listening to his moans.

"Suz, you're the best. The very best. Oh, God, oh no—"

I felt his body tense and balls tighten as his pulsing cock gushed into my mouth.

He was still semi-hard as I cleaned his dick with my tongue. I fell back and curled into his embrace, resting my head on his shoulder.

"All good?"

"You've got to be kidding. Let me say it again. Suz, you're The best! But I didn't get to do you. And we never fucked!"

"That's what tonight is for."

JERRY FELL ASLEEP WITH ONLY his feet submerged in the big Jacuzzi. I elbowed him, and he shook his head and rubbed his face.

"Watch me," I said. "Sit directly on one of the jets and then you won't drift off."

He inched his butt down to the second level.

"Okay, but it's not doing a thing for me except annoy me."

"That's because you're not a girl. It's a clit teaser. But if it keeps you awake and from drowning in three feet of bubbling hot water, then it's working."

"Are you happy, Suzanne?" He tilted his head and flashed me a questioning look.

"Very. Good home life, good job, good, uh, boyfriend. How about you?"

"Good everything."

"How is *your* home life? Is your dad around?"

"Nah, since Mom died three years ago, he's been sort of just existing. He got a girlfriend about a year ago and seems happy living with her out in western Pennsylvania."

"So where are you staying now?"

"Garden Suites, just outside of Summit. You know where. Passed the supermarket. It's comfortable and convenient."

"I'm glad, Jerry. I know exactly where Garden Suites is located. Listen, I want to tell you something interesting." I maneuvered my butt down another step to feel the bubbling warm water on my upper body. "To make a long story short, Mom told me Dad left me some money. So I went into partnership with my friend Leigh, and we bought Massage Time together. There's quite a bit of money left so I might want to go back to college and finish my degree. Anyway, that's *my* game plan."

"I'm so happy for you, Suz. But tell me your ideas for Massage Time?"

"How about at dinner I'll tell you all about Dragonfly—A Spa for Her."

"New name. I'm intrigued."

THE FOOD AT THE HOTEL WAS DELICIOUS. I had lobster and Jerry had a big sirloin steak. We shared our food and laughed at old high school stories.

"You look so sexy in that dress, Suz."

"Thank you. It's simple. A white top with spaghetti straps, a flared black skirt and a big wide black patent leather belt."

"It makes me want to eat you up—which I will do later. By the way I *am* your boyfriend and you *are* my girlfriend. It's okay to say it out loud. That's what we were in high school so that's where we're picking up, right where we left off. Starting now. We both had only a few minor interruptions, er, setbacks in between, like your flaky marriage and my—"

"Indiscretions, fucking around, poor judgment, misbehavior, stupidity—"

"Enough. At least I didn't marry any of them."

"Speaking of *them*, how is the beautiful Isa?"

"To be truthful, I haven't been with her for several months. But we're on friendly speaking terms, and she's very upset I left. So is Julia, and man, I miss that woman. I basically grew up in Dr. Unk's, and Julia was like a mother to me."

"She was like a mother to me, too. I think she took everybody under her wing who needed nurturing."

"So tell me your plan for Massage Ti…no, Dragonfly whatever?"

"Dragonfly—A Spa for Her."

"That's it. Fill me in."

"Here's an overview. We have two massage therapists so far, Javier and Steve."

I knew I was taking a big risk telling Jerry and fought back the hot blush I could tell was slowly spreading over my cheeks.

"They both have been trained in New York City, San Francisco or Europe and are certificated in—I really hate to tell you this because you'll just make fun of it—Sexological Bodywork."

His mouth opened but no words came out.

"Shall I continue?"

He nodded.

"They do a wonderful massage, sixty or ninety minutes as they talk the client through tension release, teaching them to ask for the touch they want, to notice the difference between types of touches, what they like and what they dislike. All during the massage the client is asked if the therapist can move along to another body part including the vagina. The last ten minutes can be masturbation *if* the client wishes. There are many women who have no husband, boyfriend or partner and yearn for sexual pleasure or have gynecological disorders or have experienced abuse or trauma. I'll end my little speech with Exhibit A: the Courtside Diner. That's where men can get the same thing 24/7."

Jerry looked more than surprised. He was stunned.

"Uh, Suz, uh, isn't that illegal?"

"Not if it's going on at the Courtside for men. If authorities are ignoring what's going on there, they shouldn't pay any attention to my place."

"I suppose you've got a point."

"Damn right I have. You see, I absolutely hate injustice. The unfairness of it all. We women only got the vote one hundred years ago in 1920. How long do we have to wait to have our happy endings? Another hundred? No fucking way!"

"Let me process this. Give me a little time. Okay?"

"Take all the time you need."

There seemed to be little openness to him and hardly any understanding. If he needed time, I'd give him time. I got up and walked out.

"Suz, don't go. Suz…"

His voice trailed off as I walked straight ahead and shoved hard on the metal push bar. When the door to the outside flung open, a sudden shiver sliced through me from the cool night air.

There was wood burning in a large fire pit on the

restaurant patio. A circle of people had gathered around, some singing, some making s'mores. I started to cough and needed to breathe, away from the smell of smoke and the disappointment of Jerry's response.

As I walked, I felt something on my wrist. Damn New Jersey mosquitoes. Before it bit me I raised my other hand to slap it away. Oh my God, a dragonfly.

"Well, hello. I'm so happy to see you. I want you to know I've been accepting change, investigating before making decisions and living in the present."

As soon as I said "living in the present," the dragonfly lifted straight up, did several circles in front of my face darted back and forth and flew away. I don't know if she believed me on that last one.

"I'm working on it," I yelled in its direction.

Beyond the patio were picnic tables with benches attached and a few Adirondack chairs. I sat in one, thinking it was the closest I'd get to the actual Adirondacks. Looking up at the stars, I breathed out a sigh and concentrated on identifying constellations until I felt two warm hands on my shoulders. I twisted my head around to see Jerry as he bent down and kissed me on the forehead.

"I'm sorry if I upset you, Suz. I just don't want to see you get hurt or in any trouble."

"I hope nothing happens either, but we're going to be prepared if it does."

"Actually, just thinking about it, your massage service sounds workable and practical. A woman can take her son to soccer practice, pick up her daughter's prom dress from the tailor, go to your place, get diddled, then pick up her kid after his practice, go food shopping and relax for the rest of the evening. I think I get it now." A satisfied smile appeared on his face.

"Diddled? Diddled? What the hell is that? Sounds so trivial, so demeaning."

"Well, then what about jerk off, crank and yank or a big favorite, choke the chicken? Do they sound substantive and character building to you?"

"Oh, shut up." I grabbed his hand. "Let's go back to our room and you can diddle me all you want."

Chapter Twenty-One ✕

I ADJUSTED THE WATER TEMPERATURE, piled my hair up using a big clip to keep it in place and stepped into the hotel shower. The warm spray felt calming, almost mesmerizing, as I leaned against the tile wall and closed my eyes. Jerry had been so exhausted, probably from absorbing my explanation about Dragonfly, that he fell asleep in the big blue and green plaid overstuffed chair as soon as we came back to the hotel room. I soaped and rinsed under my arms and in the folds of my pussy.

"Meow," I purred, imitating a cat, then laughed to myself thinking about Jerry and all his names for female genitalia.

"Here, kitty. Here, pretty kitty."

The shower door slid open and Jerry entered, totally naked. Oh my God, he was a breathtaking example of a man. My very own statue of David looking like Michelangelo's sculpted marble version—but mine with a very stiff erection.

"Excuse me, Miss, I thought I heard a kitty cat in here."

Jerry's sudden hand over my lady parts disarmed me as I tried to respond but only stuttered.

"Oh, look," his mouth twitched with amusement,

"here's the naughty pussy that escaped me last night."

Regrouping, I looked into his gorgeous blue eyes, "Oh, yes, I remember now," I said, almost purring. "You're the animal control officer who was looking for a lost pussy cat but fell asleep. By the way, what were you going to do with the kitty when you found her?"

"Why don't I show you?"

Sliding two of his fingers into my vagina, I gasped, then rocked back and forth on his hand as I felt my uterine muscles clench and contract.

"Don't you dare come. I want time to play with the kitty."

Jerry slowly withdrew his fingers, bent down and picked me up while capturing each one of my breasts in his mouth, suckling them, teasing my nipples and easing me downward onto one of the shower's white, built-in benches. Bending my legs up, he placed my feet beside my hips on the bench. Spreading my knees wide, he knelt in front of me.

"Now let's have a closer look at this sweet kitten."

Starting with soft kisses up and down my slit, I moaned as his tongue penetrated me and searched for all my pleasure points. I surrendered to his masterful touch as my body began to vibrate and the electricity of arousal seemed to arc through me. When his fingers on one hand opened me up, the fingers on the other hand played with my clit.

"I want to suck *you* now. Let me please, Jerry."

"Soon, baby. Soon."

Jerry's playing was replaced with his stroking my center of sensation, intense continual stroking as the fire within me increased.

"Oh my, oh, oh, oh, ah, ah ahhhh." The rush of my

climax flooded over me, and I went with it, quivering and convulsing repeatedly. Slowly coming down from my sexual mountaintop high, I felt relaxed and somewhat sleepy but Jerry's smile, growing in approval, indicated there was more to come.

"No time for basking in the glow of release. Now we'll feed the hungry cat."

He grinned as he turned off the water, picked me up and brought me into the bedroom, grabbing two big, white hotel towels along the way. Quickly drying us both, he stood me facing the front of the mirrored dresser.

Standing behind me, he remarked, "Don't we look great together? Look at yourself, perfect tits, tight tummy, beautiful ass and the face of a goddess," he said as he took each of my hands and placed them firmly on the top of the dresser. "Keep your eyes on the mirror while I give this kitten some meat to eat."

Standing behind me, he watched our reflection as he reached around and fondled my breasts, then lightly pulled and pinched my nipples. Taking his dick in one hand, Jerry rubbed it along my moist pussy before stopping at the opening. With a quick thrust of his hips, he penetrated me, then stopped as I let out a scream.

"Sorry, it's been a few years. But don't stop."

"I don't want to hurt you." He pulled out a bit, then pushed in, repeating this action until, with his last shove, he was buried balls deep.

"Oh God, that feels so good. Fill me up, Jerry. Fill me up."

"I can tell the pussy likes it. I feel the friction and suction building."

Faster and harder, faster and harder, until he

shouted, "Suzanne, you're so beautiful. I can't help it, I'm coming."

He shook and shuddered when his hands that had held my hips rose to my shoulders and collapsed over my back. I could feel his dick pulsing in me, the wetness increasing as he continued ejaculating. The juicy gush that started to drip down my inner thighs tickled and triggered something to cause a sensation in me that brought on round two.

"Don't move."

The surprise arousal built quickly going right to my clit. My arms, still on the dresser, stiffened and my backside moved back and forth, up and down, then stopped. I wanted the world to come to a halt so I could feel the crescendo of the second orgasm.

"I, I, I'm coming."

"Again?"

"Oh, oh, oh yeeeessss. Ahhgainn."

We stayed like that for a while until we pushed up on our arms and stood. Swaying, then getting my footing, I threw myself on the bed as Jerry folded himself around me.

"Wow," he said, nuzzling my neck.

"Ditto," I replied.

"Suz, do you realize that was our first fuck?"

"Our only fuck—but with three big Os."

"Are you okay with it not being in the bed?"

"Are you kidding? It wasn't ordinary. It was *extraordinary*. Totally memorable!"

"And I watched it happen in the mirror. The whole scene. Like in a movie. I loved when your body—"

"Shhh." I put my finger to my lips. "No review now. Let's get a few zzzzs."

"Okay, okay. But I'm so happy to be with you at last. I finally feel at peace, and my dick has found a home."

Slowly, his arm came around me and settled on cupping my breast. I am an independent woman but I loved feeling warm, soothed and protected—feelings Frank could never deliver. I quietly inhaled a breath and blew it out. What a difference a few months have made. From hating life to loving life. Nothing's going to ruin it now.

MY CELL PHONE RANG.

Unwinding myself from Jerry's embrace was difficult because I could tell by his steady breathing he was asleep and a deadweight. I got to the phone just in time to grab it on the last ring.

"Hello? Oh hi, Leigh. What's up?"

"Suzanne, we've got a problem."

"Tell me."

"Well, Sally had a fight with her husband and she admitted she was trying to win the argument by hurting his feelings and ended up saying she could get her loving elsewhere."

"Uh oh. What did he say?"

"Well, it seems he badgered her until she told him she had an orgasm with a massage guy. He didn't take it well but got really furious when he found out she went back for a repeat. He guessed where because ours is the only massage place around. Then he said he was going to 'make trouble and shut us the fuck down.'"

"Oh, man, in that case we're definitely on for Plan A tomorrow. Dress like we discussed, and I'll meet you at Pam's Place around six o'clock. Lots of organizing to do before it gets dark. You're on for this, right?"

"You know I am. One hundred percent. We're partners."

"Excellent. We're going to make a difference for all women, you know."

"I just hope we don't have to make it from a jail cell."

✕

"JERRY, WAKE UP. IT'S TIME TO pack up and go."

"Just let me sleep a few more minutes. Come here. Let's cuddle."

"We can't. No time."

"Well, then how about a short turn of spanking and bondage?"

"Another time. Stop stalling. I've got an emergency at work."

"What happened? No clients have orgasms today? Tell 'em to call me. I can give them a hand." He threw back his head and roared with laughter.

My annoyance vanished, as I couldn't keep myself from laughing with him.

"Yes, you are hysterically funny but this is serious. Pleeeease. I'll explain on the way."

"Okay, but since we're both naked, can we have one last hotel hug before we go back to reality?"

"I think we can squeeze that in. But no touching dicks or nipples—or pussies. Just nice hugging. Plain and simple. Agreed?"

"Yes, let's shake on it."

"Shake what? I don't trust you, Jerry Spinella."

"You can trust me, Suz." He stood up and walked a few steps toward me—with a full erection.

"Geez, does that thing ever go down?"

"Not when you're around."

I moved toward him and gave him a short sideways hug. I was sad to leave, too, and cutting short our time together.

"Obviously, this means a lot to you so I'll be a good boy and pack up. But first I want to be close and feel you next to me. How's that sound?"

"Great. Two minutes." I saw the heart-rending tenderness of his gaze and melted. "Standing, not in bed."

In one forward motion, I locked myself in his arms and reached up, burying my hands in his thick hair.

With a soft breath he whispered in my ear, "I love you, Suzanne, and not just the sex."

Time stopped. I wanted to pause and remember his words exactly. My response flowed naturally as if I had always known what it would be.

"I love you, too, Jerry. Since forever."

Looking into his deep blue eyes, I raised myself to meet his lips. His kiss was warm and sweet as we both savored every moment, his hold firm but much too inviting. At last we reluctantly parted and began packing.

After tossing our things into his truck, he said, "I don't want to go."

"Me neither, and I'm so sorry, Jerry. It's been the best for me—and my pussy." I patted the area of my jeans between my legs and chuckled with happy memories.

149

"See, you've gotten quite used to that word. Shall we try for twat or cunt next week?"

"Slow up, sweets. Next week is jam-packed with quelling a revolt and starting a revolution."

"Holy shit, Suz, you better fill me in."

"I like it even better when you fill me up."

Chapter Twenty-Two ⨉

I GAZED OUT THE TRUCK WINDOW on our way back to Summit, bracing to divulge my Plan A, but got sidetracked remembering how just a short time ago I was making love with Jerry for the first time. And also heard him say "I love you" for the first time. Was he thinking something similar as we drove? I was certain that I was in love with him and always had been. But there were just a few things I needed to check out.

Jerry broke the silence. "So, Suz, tell me about the big emergency and why we had to leave so abruptly."

"Will do, but it's a bit of a ride so I have one more question for you."

"Haven't I answered all of your questions to your satisfaction?"

"I just want to make sure we have no secrets between us."

"Whatever. Shoot."

"Did you ever have sex with two or multiple girls at Dr. Unk's?"

"What do you mean, multiple?"

"You know very well what I mean. One, two, four, five, six, etc. And remember the truth will set you free."

"Free? I don't feel like a captive. But okay, yes, I

151

did. I think it was three but there could have been a fourth. There, I said it."

"Did you like it?"

"What's not to like? Four or more hands on your dick are pretty exciting. But, listen, Suz, it's not the same or even as sexually arousing as being with you. It doesn't matter how many women you screw at one time. It's meaningless. Frankly, fucking with multiples can be exhausting, and you have to go through the motions to be a people pleaser and make everyone happy. In the end you quickly exit when it's over."

"I believe you, Jerry, but how can I know that you won't be screwing with all the people that work out at your new gym or at least be fucking them in your mind? So many women I know are sleeping with their professional trainers where they exercise. My girlfriends tell me those places are 'meat markets.'"

"When your heart is into someone, you don't want to ruin a relationship by being unfaithful. You want to be everything for that person and to have that person be all for you. That said, as a human being, you can't help but admire good bodies and faces. I think the same goes for women. Now my turn to hear *your* secret?"

"Ask me anything."

"This place you have, Dragonfly, did you ever partake in the services offered? In other words, were you a client?"

"You mean did I ever get diddled?"

"Did you ever get an extended massage culminating in masturbation by a man—or two—or three?"

"The answer is yes. But you have to understand it

was very clinical. The massage therapist, just one, spoke softly throughout the whole session, explaining what was happening. I did it twice during the several weeks *before* you came back into my life. I hadn't had sex or a facsimile thereof for three years with my ex. The only love I received was from my dog. But, really, what's so different from me having an orgasm at Dragonfly and you having an orgy at Dr. Unk's?"

"When you think about it, not much. If we're dating now, can I have exclusive diddling privileges?"

"Absolutely. And can I count on you not drooling over every girl on the treadmill in your gym and then doing her in the trainer's office?"

"I promise."

"First, I want to hug you and kiss you," I said, leaning over and winding my hand behind Jerry's neck.

Turning around and boosting myself up on my knees, I kissed his cheek and spread kisses down his neck while he was driving.

"Oh, man, you smell just like yourself, and I love it." I felt a hand on my breast and a quick nipple tweak.

"Suz, you are the one I've waited for all these years, and I don't want to share you with anyone else. Your kisses tell me you feel the same way."

"Yes, I want us to develop a strong and honest relationship. I will be there for you, and I want you to be there for me."

"Absolutely. Now tell me your plans for the revolt or revolution or whatever you're doing."

"It's time there was a revolution because the whole situation is revolting and has been for a long

153

time. Centuries and centuries and centuries."

"I get your point, Suz. Going on for a long time. But bring me up to speed. Now. Currently. Today."

"How many times do we need to see this historically themed movie—even today?" I sat back and folded my arms. "The tired premise: The little woman busy with the kids, cooking and cleaning while the man goes out and brings home the kill or, better yet, more than his kill. Sound cavemanish? That's because it happened that way then and still goes on every day now.

"Back to the old movie. And because the poor guy is so exhausted from the hunt, and hanging out with the boys, he goes and gets a happy ending from a woman in a neighboring cave and pays her with some squirrel meat. Can women do the same? No way. No happy ending for her. Why? Because we're supposed to wait around for a knight in shining armor? Fuck that crap. It's because women are still in many ways second-class citizens or, worse, thought of as property. Bottom line: Women don't matter as much as men."

"But we have to protect women or they'll be preyed on by lecherous males just waiting to take advantage of them."

"Bull shit. We can take care of ourselves. Think of the #MeToo movement. Women working together to make men face up to their offenses against women."

"Okay, so what *do* women want?"

"Full sexual equality."

"I guess this means no trying bondage or handcuffs."

"Yes, but this time we'll put them on you."

"Shit. No thanks."

"See?"

"I get it but you're scaring me. I didn't know you were so militant."

"Have you ever known me to run away from anything?"

"Yeah, me."

"Oh, right. Sorry. I wasn't thinking straight back then. But how about being proud of me now for trying to right an injustice? Just one injustice occurring in two neighboring New Jersey towns. I'm not talking about changing the whole world's attitude and publicizing it on the evening news—that's for next week. Just joking."

I couldn't resist curling into a ball, holding my stomach laughing.

"So I need to be with a strong man who can be a good sexual partner as well as understand and support me. Can you do that?"

"Here's my answer: I like giving you a happy ending better than getting one."

"Good start."

JERRY PULLED THE TRUCK UP in front of my house.

"But you didn't get to tell me your detailed plan."

"Later, babe. There's a show and tell component," I said in a low voice as Mom came running out to greet us. "Tell you what. I'll come to your room in Garden Suites before work around eight o'clock tomorrow morning so we can discuss it then. Okay?"

"A morning booty call," he grinned. "Can't turn it down."

"Did you have a good time?" Mom was bubbling

155

over with excitement.

"We had a great time, didn't we, Jerry?"

"Confusing but the best."

"Confusing?" Of course, Mom would pick up on that word.

"Your daughter has some interesting ideas about fighting an injustice."

"That's my girl."

Whoa! Thanks, Mom.

"I guess I'm outnumbered," Jerry mumbled.

"Nope. Equal opportunity here. Buddy's a male. That makes two against two. Please stay for dinner, Jerry. You can help cook the hamburgers on the grill. And I made mac and cheese. I remember that's your favorite."

"I'd love to stay. Okay with you, Suz?"

"Of course. More time to look at my handsome guy."

Our eyes met and I could feel the chemistry. It had always been there. What the hell was wrong with me choosing Frank? And for an instant my mind went down the hole I had just crawled out of.

"Okay, kids, let's finish up the prep work so we can eat."

I could tell Mom was on a roll and happy about Jerry coming into my life again.

Jerry put his arm around me and pulled me into him as we walked out through the kitchen to the patio. I loved the shower of his affection as much as the big-time sex. Well, almost as much.

"Suz, watch and learn as I make these burgers."

"Do you know what you're doing? You didn't cook at Dr. Unk's."

"No, but I looked and listened to the cooks. Uh oh, don't move. You've got a big bug on your shoulder."

Jerry's hand reached down to swat the insect away but I put my arm out mid-bug crush.

"Stop, that's a dragonfly. Don't hurt it. It eats other annoying insects like mosquitoes."

Putting my hand up toward my shoulder, the dragonfly flew onto my fingers.

"Suzanne, that's amazing, Ask it a question." Mom had totally bought into this "insect as a fortune teller thing."

"Should I feel compelled to right a wrong as I see it?"

The dragonfly took flight and shimmered as its blue and green iridescent wings fluttered, landing back on my hand.

"I'll take that as a yes. Another question: Or should I stay and take care of my massage business?

The insect's wings drooped as it fell on its back, legs in the air.

"So that's a no. Well then, should I go to law school?"

Going straight up like a helicopter, the dragonfly circled my head three times, dove and pulled up to eye level, then zipped off into the night.

"A resounding yes. I knew it, I knew it. My wish has come true." Jumping up and down, Mom clapped nonstop. "And I'm sure that dragonfly has more wisdom to share. You just wait and see."

"Mom, calm down."

"I think the dragonfly knows you better than you know yourself," Jerry chimed in.

"You, too, Jerry? I can tell you're both believers.

It's just an insect. Hello!"

We heard a ringing sound, and all of us pulled out our phones. It was Jerry's.

"Hello. Julia? So great to hear your voice. What's up?" He turned away and went into the house.

Mom and I finished everything else and managed not to burn the burgers. A few minutes later Jerry returned and sat down with us at the patio table.

"I thought Julia was going to give me a list of problems at the bar but she said the most amazing thing. She's leaving now that the sale has gone through, and she wants to make a move to North Jersey—to be near us."

"Oh, how wonderful. That would be great. We can help her get settled."

"And she's bringing Isa with her," he said, breaking into a broad smile.

Chapter Twenty-Three ✕

I KNOCKED.

Jerry threw open the door to his motel suite, naked. "Uh, who the hell are you?"

"It's me, Suzanne. I'm in disguise. Great, you didn't recognize me."

"Say what?"

I took off my baseball cap and shook out my hair. "See. It's me."

"Shit, Suz, how to give a guy a heart attack."

"You? What about me? Answering the door nude."

"You said you were coming over, and I saw your car go around the building from the side window. I wanted to surprise you in my new suit."

"Jerry, you don't have a thing on. What suit?"

"The suit I got for my birthday. A little small at first but I grew into it."

"Ah, yes, I get it. You certainly did surprise me but now that I see it on you, I like it. I like it a lot. Especially the buttons." I tweaked his nipples. "And the tailoring. So form fitting. Perfect for your slim, trim body."

I ran my hands up and down his well defined manly chest, his sides and around his waist.

"But there's one thing I can't figure out."

"What's that?"

"Why does it have a handle on the front?"

"It's built-in. It comes with the suit."

"What do you do with it?"

"It works like a barometer. It tells me if I'm turned on."

"Then what happens?"

"It's like a heat-seeking missile. It raises up and guides itself into home port."

"Niiiice. Then what are those things hanging behind it?"

"Balls."

"What for?"

"To play with when I'm bored."

"I'D LOVE TO GIVE YOU A BLOW job but I have to get to work," I said, checking my watch. "I came over this morning to see if you thought I looked convincing as a young man. It's my disguise for tonight. Leigh and I are going undercover at the Courtside—"

"You're whaaat?"

"It's a long story but Dragonfly has been accidentally outed to the County Sheriff. How long we'll be able to stay in business is unknown. So, to buy some protective measures, we're going to photograph and record what goes on for men underneath the Courtside Diner. The old 'what's good for the goose is good for the gander' defense.'"

Cringing, I looked at Jerry's face for some sign of understanding.

He surprised me. "Crazy but makes sense. Can I

help? I have a penis, does that count?"

"And such a fine one but we know what we need and we'll take it from our perspective. But hold on, perhaps you can wait outside the door and, as Leigh and I come out, we can surreptitiously pass you our phones. I don't want to go through this whole surveillance thing and then have our evidence confiscated."

"I'm your man. Where and when do we meet?"

"Tonight, Pam's Place, six o'clock."

"Just one taste of this beauty," I said, my hand on Jerry's chest pushing him onto the bed. With my eyes focused on his face and my hand wrapped around his cock, I lowered my mouth to cover the thick head of his hard-on and sucked down deep. After another big lick up and down his shaft, tracing the length of him with my wet, hot tongue, I jumped up, ran out the door and yelled, "Rain check later tonight. Promise."

BY THE TIME I GOT TO WORK, the phones were already ringing. I recorded several appointments, made some coffee for the women who were waiting and put on some lipstick and blush after going barefaced earlier to look like a boy. Leigh rushed in and signaled to me to come over to the coffee corner.

"Three things. Here's your mustache for tonight," she said, peeling what looked like one of two dead caterpillars off a tiny piece of paper. "I'm giving you the smaller one because you're blonde and shorter than me."

"Good idea, thanks. And what's the second thing?"

Leigh went behind the front desk and brought out an armful of material that turned out to be two lightweight hoodies. One black and one navy blue, both extra large. "These are to hide more of our faces but mainly to cover our boobs. Wear your baseball cap, then put this over it and pull the drawstring. With the mustaches and, oh, here's some lightly darkened sunglasses, we'll be unrecognizable."

"Wow, Leigh, you really thought this caper through visually. Thanks so much for being such a great collaborator. Now what's the third thing?"

"Two more massage guys are coming to interview at half past three today. Can you be here?"

"Absolutely. Wouldn't miss it. Hey, how's Steve doing?"

A dreamy look crossed her face. "Fabulous. What if I want to date him?"

"You date him. Chemistry is chemistry. But aren't you a bit older?"

"Yeah. Isn't that wonderful?"

"Doesn't he want children?"

"He already has one. A daughter who lives in Morristown with her mother. He visits on weekends. It's one reason he wanted to move here from the city."

"That's nice. Sounds like he's a good dad. Guess what? Morristown is the place Jerry and I ended up this past weekend. It's a pretty area."

"Did you two get over the hump of the first fuck?"

"Not only that but he said the 'L' word."

"I'm so happy for you, Suzanne. Your life is really on an uptick. And the sex was good, too?"

"Jerry says I'm the orgasm queen. Although I told him *all* about our business at Dragonfly, I didn't explain how being coached by Javier gave me an edge up in bed. In other words, I knew how to ask for what I needed and how to physically position myself to get the results I wanted."

"Actually, Suzanne, that's a good sales pitch for Dragonfly. We are a clinical school where women can learn what to ask their husbands/partners/lovers for in the sack."

"From the number of phones calls, sounds like our clients are already doing the sales pitching to others."

AT PROMPTLY HALF PAST THREE THE TWO MEN interviewing for the position as our next massage therapist came through the glass doors. They introduced themselves as Ricky and Marty. Ricky was at least six feet tall, lean and had dark hair pulled back in a shoulder-length ponytail. He had a sculptured face and his cut jaw had a slight stubble. He wore a black leather motorcycle jacket over a tight white t-shirt and black jeans.

Marty's skin was a light caramel color, and his dark hair was neck-length with lightened streaks and pushed back behind his ears. He was a few inches shorter than Ricky but his muscles were bulked up; he obviously lifted weights. He wore a jeans jacket over a black t-shirt and faded Levi's with a black belt.

Both men knew Javier and Steve, and all greeted each other with manly hugs and handshakes. Leigh and I took a seat on the couch in the lobby, and the men drew up chairs around us. They both gave satisfactory answers until I asked my last, most revealing question: "Are you willing to take on any woman as a client who makes an appointment, no matter who or what?"

"Absolutely," Ricky quickly volunteered. "I'm anxious to work with any woman who wants help to release tension and learn about her own sexuality."

"Me, too," Marty echoed his friend but added, "I do short, I do tall, I do thin, but I don't do fat."

We all sat in silence.

"Well, I gotta be honest. Unless she wants the third arm." He slapped his knees and bent over laughing.

Leigh and I did a double take, our eyes widening when his words sunk in.

"And we appreciate your honesty, Marty."

Javier quickly stood and shook their hands and thanked them for coming. He knew Leigh and I were unhinged and at a loss for words so he took over the final goodbyes.

"We'll give you a call in the next few days. We're not sure if we want to hire two men or just one. There's been a few client requests for a female massage therapist, and we should consider that need, too."

By that time Leigh and I got our act together and walked them both to the door, thanking them for making the trip from New York City.

After they left, we all just looked at each other. Shaking our heads in disbelief at hearing blatant fat shaming, we agreed we'd hire Ricky but not Marty.

LEIGH AND I ZOOMED THROUGH all of Dragonfly's closing duties to get to Pam's Place by six o'clock. My phone signaled a text had come through. One glance made me smile. It was Julia. She was in the area now and wanted to stop by Dragonfly before going to her motel. I texted back to come anytime. Five minutes went by and I looked up. There she was at the glass doors. I ran to let her inside and get my hug.

Julia was the world's best female hugger. Her hold was warm, firm and comforting, like a big bear hug minus the claws and teeth. Feeling safe and protected, I wanted to stay in her arms longer but could see behind her someone was standing alone in the empty doorway.

Isa was striking with her seductive young body and wild beauty. Her hair was a long, dark cascade of lose shiny curls flowing over her shoulders and down her back. Her skin was the shade of coffee latte, and her face, beautiful at first, became even more stunning as one lingered on her dark almond-shaped eyes, long eyelashes and full lips. No wonder Jerry probably fucked her like crazy and, with his head between her legs, slurped up her cunt juices.

The green-eyed monster in me is on the prowl.

Leigh, Javier and Steve came out from the back and announced all the rooms had been cleaned and sanitized. I introduced them to Julia and Isa and asked Leigh if she was ready to go to Pam's Place. She nodded in agreement. As I gathered my clothing for my disguise, I noticed Javier and Isa had moved off toward the coffee corner. Leaning in, I could hear them conversing in Spanish. Too bad I majored in French and Latin in high school, but figured out enough to understand Javier saying, "Free massage for you."

SALLY RAN UP TO US AS WE entered the restaurant.

"I'm sooo sorry. Me and my big mouth." She had tears in her eyes and tried to hug us each repeatedly. "You know I wouldn't hurt your business on purpose. I'm just so frustrated with Don. He always has to have the last word, and he always has to be right."

"Don't worry, Sally. Speaking up to your husband probably gave Leigh and me the boot in the butt we needed to take action. Dry those tears and meet my boyfriend Jerry."

They shook hands. "My, he's so handsome. Where have you been hiding him?"

"Under her bed," he said, giving Sally an eye roll with a grin.

"So Jerry," she changed the subject, a bit embarrassed, "are you going to help Leigh and Suzanne with whatever their secret plan is for tonight?"

"No, I'm just driving the getaway car."

Chapter Twenty-Four ✈

I PUT MY HANDS OVER MY MOUTH to cover an oncoming sneeze. The bushes by the Courtside Diner's backdoor tickled my nose, or was it the tiny fake mustache? Crouching down, I could sense Jerry's tall legs standing behind me. He reached down and rubbed my back. I looked up and blew him a secret kiss as the door opened and three men staggered out. Several car doors opened in the parking lot, and three men went in as Leigh and I followed, slipping inside after them.

Game on!

Pasting ourselves against the white wall in a long hallway with a succession of white doors spaced every ten feet or so, we saw each man enter a separate room. When all the doors were closed, I whispered to Leigh that I was going to "accidentally" open one and walk in, pretending, as a teenager, I didn't know the Courtside-massage-happy-ending drill. At that point she should take a quick photo of the scene inside as we immediately ducked out and ran fast. But first, we needed to give it about fifteen or twenty minutes before the massages finished and the happy endings began.

There was one folding chair further down the hallway. Leigh took a seat, and I bent down beside her.

When three more men entered the building, she sank lower in her chair as we pulled the drawstrings of our hoodies even tighter.

I thought about what a young man would say or do in this instance. In a lowered but not quiet voice, I told Leigh maybe we should go.

"Don't get scared now. We've come this far," she answered, pitching her voice as low as she could.

"This your first time?" a short man in a blue plaid shirt nearest Leigh asked. "You'll like it if you stay. Very relaxing. You can go in as soon as the next man comes out."

"I don't think anyone's in the room across from us," I said, pointing directly to the door. "Let's go see."

"Hold it," blue plaid shirt guy said. "Not good to open it if someone's in there."

Giving Leigh the sharp elbow, we both rose and walked toward the door. I grabbed the doorknob and yanked. Phone in hand, Leigh clicked off several photos in succession. A fast scan of the room showed me all I needed to know. A naked man lying face up on the table with a topless woman leaning over him giving him a hand job. As we turned to run, the agile guy on the table flipped his bare feet to the ground and was close behind us. Hearing his short, heavy breaths behind us as we ran down the hallway and approached the door to the outside, Leigh stopped, turned and took pictures of him.

Flinching and flinging up his hands to hide his face, he yelled. "Are you some private dicks? Don't tell my wife. Please."

"Too bad," I shouted back, "she'll recognize that

pint-sized penis anywhere."

Handing off our phones to Jerry was easy with all the chaos and commotion going on as we beat it to his truck.

"Drive," I said emphatically as we all jumped in and made sure the door locks were down.

"Wait," Jerry whispered, taking the truck out of gear and putting it in park. "Get a load of what's happening by those hedges. See there. Under the streetlight."

As we looked three men in suits with disheveled shirts and loosened ties climbed out of a white limousine zipping up their pants. Three women in skimpy shorts, low cut glittery tank tops and fuck-me type spiked high heels came out next. All six of them gathered close together near the hedges as the men forked over what looked like fistfuls of money to the women. A man in a chauffer's cap came around from the driver's side of the limo, held out his hand and was given cash as well.

"Hey," I squinted and pointed. "Isn't that the government official that was on the front page of yesterday's paper? The one who gained contracts to replace the aging lead water pipes in many northern New Jersey towns?"

"Suz, how can you tell?" Jerry asked. "I can't see that far in this dim light."

"Easy to identify by his slicked back white hair, and the big dark streak he has in it going all the way from front to back. The reverse skunk look. I've read about it. It's his signature hairdo. He's that terrible legislator who has some kind of business located in South Jersey and won the low bid to complete the replacement project. Except everything's gone wrong, for which he takes no blame and keeps increasing the cost to fix his own fuck-ups. Supposedly, according to the television news, he's getting signed affidavits from the legislators in North Jersey stating his legitimacy and professional work."

I pushed open the truck door and ran to the scene, whispering, "Another great photo op," over my shoulder.

Jerry, my personal protector, leapt from his truck, yelling, "I told you not to come anywhere near this place, uh, Junior. You're going to be punished. Big time."

As I got closer, my best option was to just aim and shoot. All seven people turned toward the disturbance, searching to see in the dark but, fortunately were blinded enough to look directly my way, deer in headlights style. Jerry came running and swooped me up. Carrying me back to the truck, he shouted for all to hear, "Son, you're gonna get it when we get home. Wait till your mother finds out."

Jerry threw me in the passenger seat. "Stay there, Junior," he yelled for good measure as he gunned the engine, rumbled over a speed bump and drove out of the Courtside Diner's back parking lot.

Couldn't help it. I laughed at myself, at Leigh and Jerry, at our insane teenage disguises and at the crazy circumstances. We all laughed until we had no more laughter left in us.

"Now what?" Leigh said. "I know, ice cream for everyone, my treat at Pam's Place, to review and analyze tonight plus see what photos we've got on our phones."

"I know what I want," Jerry said, grabbing my hand.

Leaning into him, I whispered, "Later, babe. For sure."

"Shut up."

"No, you shut up."

"No, *you* shut up."

"I'll say it one more time, Sally. Men have needs."

"Needs. Schmeeds. And women don't?"

"Not like men."

"Oh really, Don? You got a clit?"

"No, a dick. It's biology. Pressure builds up and it needs release. Often."

We came into the restaurant and stood by the door. "Did you overhear all that?" With Sally's folded arms and pissed off face, we got the picture.

"So sorry," I said. "We don't want to disturb you. Just some ice cream and then we're good to go—if you're not closing yet."

"This way," she pointed toward the corner table. "I just made a fresh pot of coffee if anybody's interested."

"That's great, Sally. Thanks."

Adrenaline that had gotten me to this point was beginning to slide. We all took a seat. Leigh and I pulled off our hoods and mustaches but kept our baseball hats on.

"Now let's see what we have on our phones."

Leigh clicked through her photos. She had some good ones of the naked man getting a hand job, then running down the hall chasing us. Also she snapped some of the other men who came in and went into the rooms for a massage and happy ending. My phone had captured the limousine, the disheveled men, the call girls and the driver.

"These pictures ought to do it." I was sure of our defense. "This is our hedge against Dragonfly being closed down."

"I wonder—"

"Wonder what, Jerry?"

"I wonder if those men in the limo were the legislators from the north being treated to 'a sex night on the town' to sweeten the deal of signing affidavits attesting to the good replacement of the lead water pipes?"

"Whoa, Jerry, I think you've nailed their fraudulent scheme. I'm sure more money is also changing hands."

"Ice cream, everyone," Sally said as she put huge bowls of the cold stuff in front of each of us.

Leigh's eyebrows shot up. "I can't eat all this."

"No doggie bags for ice cream." Sally replied, then came around the table to me. "Shhh," Sally whispered in my ear as she bent down and put a spoon by my dish of ice cream. "Don's going to make a raid on your place around noon tomorrow. Just letting you know."

"Thank you, Sally. Looks yummy," I said, sounding like I was thanking her for the strawberry and chocolate chip ice cream.

As soon as we got into the truck, I told Jerry and Leigh about Don the County Sheriff and his plan. No worries, I assured them, because we now had evidence of what really was going on behind the Courtside

Diner. With that proof we could pull the sexual inequality card for Dragonfly. They agreed but said they wouldn't let me face the Sheriff alone and would be at Dragonfly at noon.

"But wait a sec," Leigh interrupted. "Do you think those women giving the massages and happy endings are possibly trafficked? You know, exploited for the money they make giving sexual service?"

"Whoa, Leigh, you could be right. That's a question the Sheriff better be able to answer."

After we dropped Leigh off at her real estate office, Jerry drove me back to his room at the Garden Suites to pick up my car. "How about staying overnight with me?"

He looked so hopeful I couldn't say no. Nor did I want to.

I texted Mom not to expect me tonight and I would see her tomorrow—another small reach for independence that gave me confidence I could tackle tomorrow's problem at Dragonfly and win.

"MY PLACE, MY RULES." Jerry gave me a grin that sent my pulse racing.

"So that's the way you're going to play it?"

"You bet."

We tore off our clothes, unbuttoning, unsnapping, untying and unzipping everything until we were totally naked. Jerry pulled me in. His sudden move made my nipples ache and my breath hitch. Slowly and teasingly, he kissed the narrow line of my jaw, down the side of my neck and over the bend of my shoulder. Oh, man, I was halfway there.

I slid my hand down and found his thick, hard cock. "Please let me—"

"Not yet," he pushed my hand away and palmed my breasts. Gently sucking each one, he pinched and pulled my nipples until they hardened, then worked his way down to my navel, licking a trail with his moist tongue. Hopefully, my moaning told him the prolonged anticipation was becoming unbearable.

"Jerry, I—"

The tip of his tongue slipping past my lips and tracing the edges of my teeth cut me off. As the kiss grew in intensity, our tongues were dancing and I wanted more. And nothing was enough. Writhing and grinding my body into his, the feelings of arousal were almost painful.

Jerry lowered his mouth between my thighs.

"Suz, you are so beautiful. I want all of you."

Sliding his hand down past my pubic bone, he opened my moist folds and licked upwards. Long, slow strokes over and over before he pressed his thumb to my nub of nerve endings. The licking and sudden circular motion of his middle finger on my clit caused uncontrollable body spasms and vaginal pulsing too strong to suppress.

"Oh, God, Jerry. I'm coming."

The climax ripped through me like a category 4 hurricane. Every muscle tightened as I convulsed, shuddered and shivered again and again. Afterward I lay in silent contentment, then sat up.

"Wait, what about *your* orgasm? A suck or a fuck?"

"Both."

"Right. Your place, your rules."

"Lie face up on the bed sideways and hang your head over the edge."

Standing behind my head, Jerry came close and put his enlarged dick in between my lips.

"Oh, yeah, fuck my mouth" were the last garbled words I got out before his stroking, then thrusting, took over.

"Oh, God, Suz, you take it so deep. But now I want to fuck your cunt before I come. Get on top. Straddle me."

After a quick switch of positions, I lowered myself onto his straining, erect cock.

"Fill me up. Yes. So thick."

I could feel my inner walls stretch and clench as he guided his big dick in and through my wetness into the center of my being.

"Ride me, Suz, ride me."

And I did. Until I heard his groans and grunts as he emptied himself into me. Cradling his balls, I sucked down his remaining cum, remembering the delicious taste from high school that was even better now.

His eyes met mine. "I love you, Suz. I want this, what we have together. Always."

"Me, too. I love you, Jerry. Forever."

I woke up in the middle of the night feeling lonely and alone—residual and familiar emotions from all the empty nights with Frank. Jerry slept soundly with his broad naked back facing me. I wanted to wake him and ask him to turn toward me for a front contact hug to soothe and comfort me to sleep. But instead, I turned my bare back to him and inched closer and closer. Finally, there was no space between us, the small of my back fitting perfectly into the rugged, taut slope of his mid-back. I could feel the heat of his body as it penetrated and worked its way down the entire length of me. And I knew, more than ever, this was my home.

Chapter Twenty-Five ✕

WE STOOD IN THE DOORWAY of Jerry's room in Garden Suites. Taking my wrist, he pulled my hand to his lips. Kissing the open palm, he looked into my eyes. "I wish you the best today, and I will see you at noon. Don't do or say anything inflammatory, at least until I get there. No, I'm not showing up to save you. You have the balls," he chuckled, "I mean, the Jersey grit to see this through. I'm just backup. That's all."

"I got myself into this predicament, and I have to get myself out. Hopefully, my surefire strategy with facts and photos will work. And if not, I have a secret good luck charm just in case. Something to protect me from evil spirits. One last kiss, Jerry," I grinned, "before the Sheriff hauls me off to jail."

I leaned in. He leaned in. One of his hands slid down into the back of my jeans and cupped my ass. As I pulled back, I looked up. then we locked gazes. No time for sex now but I wanted this kiss to embody all my loving feelings for him with none of the tentative uncertainty I had when we first rekindled our relationship. All those uneasy thoughts like: Is he leading me on? Does he have feelings for me? Is he in love with someone else? What are his intentions? Does he think I'm just going to be a fuck buddy? What the hell am I doing? But no kiss ever had all the answers. It was when I plunged in and took a "kiss risk" that produced the capacity just to enjoy the received kiss and give kissing pleasure that quelled those unsure doubts that could've ruined our relationship.

Jerry understood my need and gently lowered his mouth onto my waiting lips. As the scent of his natural manliness broke through the faint smell of his spicy aftershave, I smothered a groan and instinctively parted my lips. His kiss wasn't insistent but warm and sweet, giving me a chance to stop short and remember today's mission.

Withdrawing his hand from my jeans, he moved back from our loving see-you-later kiss.

"Not one day of jail time for my Suz. No Sheriff is taking away the woman who gives me the best sex, ever."

"First things first. Right?"

"You got it, babe." At that point Jerry lightly kissed the tip of my nose, my eyes and then my forehead. "Goodbye, sweetheart. I'll see you at noon. Love you."

"Love you, too."

I walked to my van parked by the motel's fence that bordered a wooded lot, thinking how I hit the boyfriend jackpot this time.

"Wait." Jerry's voice yelled through the distance. "What magic charm?"

Turning back, I shouted, "You'll see."

I CRANKED OVER THE ENGINE and looked behind me before I put my van in reverse to back out of my parking space. I stopped. It looked like a leaf was pasted on my windshield. I got out to inspect it. Nothing moved—until it did. I gasped. A dead dragonfly. Or was it dead? The wings were oddly askew. One set grew out from the body horizontally as usual. The other set went straight up vertically, perhaps knocked out of alignment. Then I noticed all four wings were faintly fluttering.

"Oh, you poor thing. What can I do to help?"

The buzzing sound of the wings increased.

"How about if I lift you up and put you down in the woods?"

Louder buzzing, almost as if it was angry with my suggestion.

"Well, then how about if I leave you on my windshield and drive you slowly to my mother's house?"

The buzzing stopped.

"I'll take that as a yes. Hang on tight."

I carefully drove onto the highway, taking each turn with care and cautiously keeping my eye on the insect and on the road. As I neared Mom's house and turned into the driveway, I realized the dragonfly's wings against my van's windshield were in the shape of a perfect L. I cut the engine and jumped out.

"This is all about *love*, isn't it?"

Extending my fingers toward the dragonfly, the insect turned itself over and crawled onto my hand.

With my arm outstretched, I walked to the field in the backyard. The buzzing began again. No, I guess not. I changed direction and thought about where the dragonfly needed to be. Then I remembered. Moving ever so gently, I reached the water-filled, hand-painted pedestal ceramic birdbath.

"Here you are, little dragonfly. Rest here on the edge and get a drink of water."

I put it down as I watched the wings return to their natural horizontal position with two on one side and two on the other. As the buzzing increased, the dragonfly took off, skimmed across the birdbath and lifted into the air.

"You faker!" I laughed and shook my head. "Got it. All about love. Right?"

The answer came in three twirls above my head, a deep dive pulling up in front of my face, then zigzagging left and right and darting off into the woods. Still laughing, I waved goodbye.

TURNING AND FACING THE BACK of Mom's house, the smell of pancakes cooking wafted out from the open kitchen window. Going around to the front door, I let myself in with my key.

"Hey, Mom," I yelled, "am I in time for a short stack?"

Reaching the doorway to the kitchen, I heard footsteps and collided into a tall man in a burgundy-colored terry cloth bathrobe. "Oh, oh, sorry. I, uh, I—"

Mom, in a matching bathrobe, rushed between us.

"Well, this is awkward. John, meet my daughter, Suzanne."

I waited a few seconds to get control of my breathing, then stuck out my hand. Obviously embarrassed, he cautiously returned the handshake. John was tall and built like an older version of a football player. He had a ruddy complexion and a warm, but somewhat confused, smile that didn't quite reach his clear brown eyes. His high and tight haircut, I supposed, was for convenience as a policeman.

"I'm just here to get some clothes. Don't let me keep you from your breakfast."

"All right, Suzanne, but after you get your things, come down and have some pancakes with us."

"Will do," I replied as I ran upstairs.

Shutting my door, I threw myself on the bed, wondering if I could deal with my mother having a boyfriend. And matching bathrobes? Really! But what about Dad? The thought came to me that this whole cozy kitchen scene was one of the things I learned about in Al-Anon. To accept the things I cannot change. Dad was dead. Period. I cannot change that. And acceptance of Mom wanting to find love. I needed to accept that, too. Yes, life moves on. Surely, Dad wouldn't want Mom to be lonely for the rest of her life. Mom met John at an Al-Anon meeting, and both gained the courage to move on together. Good for them. I accept that. At least I'll work on it.

It is all about love. Right, little dragonfly?

Before I dressed and went downstairs, I made a call and left a message.

"Help! You have what I need. Meet me at the Dragonfly spa at 11:30. Please."

Now what to put on? Quickly searching my closet, I knew I didn't want anything frilly, showing cleavage, short or colorful. It needed to be plain and to the point. I pulled out a black, lightweight jersey, calf-length jewel neck, sleeveless dress that made me look tall and, I hoped, a bit threatening. I added strappy high black sandals and wound my hair into a bun to give me an even more serious, professional look. I checked the mirror on the back of my closet door.

Perfect!

Running downstairs, I glanced into the kitchen.

"Gotta get to work. So nice to meet you, John. Next time I'll have more time to chat."

"Why are you in that outfit for work?"

Mom and her "why" questions.

Almost thirty, with nothing to hide, it was time to be totally honest. "Truth is I am meeting with the Sheriff. I heard he is going to try to close down my massage spa. I need to *look* stern and *sound* firm."

John spoke up. "I know him. Be careful. He can be a real bastard. But he folds easily if you have facts on your side."

"I think we do, but thanks for the info. I'll keep it in mind."

"Good luck," he said with a sincere smile. "But watch out for the dog."

Chapter Twenty-Six ✗

DOG? WHAT DOG? SALLY NEVER SAID she and Don had a pet. Just in case, on the way out, I grabbed a box of Buddy's mini-sized dog biscuits Mom kept in the garage. You never know.

As I drove I mentally reviewed my new and improved plan. My phone rang. I glanced at the screen.

"Leigh," I said, picking up, "everything all right?"

"Yes, we're all here and ready. It's half past eleven. Half an hour until the Sheriff shows."

"Tell me who's there."

"Well, me, Javier, Steve, Ricky and Jerry's just walked in."

"Great. But just to let you know the plan has changed."

"I didn't know there was a plan."

"Well, it's good you didn't because it's changed. Tell everyone to hang in; I'll be there in ten minutes."

Outside, the sun had broken through the sheet of clouds and the fine mist that had fallen overnight was clearing up. The temperature was moving upward. Combined with my racing pulse, I could feel my face becoming hot. A quick glance in my rear-view mirror showed me my cheeks were flushed. I pulled into a space and quickly parked. Taking the elevator up to the

Dragonfly spa, I wondered if the Sheriff would ride up or try to conquer the circular stairway. Getting out, I heard voices coming from below. I knew that voice. I looked down the stairs.

"Julia. Thank God you're here!"

"So, Chicken Little, is the sky falling? I came as fast as I could after I got your voicemail," she said, jogging up the last few steps. "I brought Isa. Hope that's okay."

"Perfect," I replied. "Hi, Isa," I said, glad she had her eye on Javier now and off *my* Jerry. "Go ahead inside, Isa. I need to talk to Julia for a few minutes."

"Here's the deal, Julia." I told her about the clinical massages that were being done very professionally at Dragonfly and about the massages with happy endings that were going on behind the Courtside Diner. I also told her about how Leigh and I dressed up as teenagers and took pictures of the activities there. And about the Sheriff's rage at learning his wife was partaking in our massages and his determination to "shut us the fuck down."

"And what do you need from me, exactly?"

"You took no shit at Dr. Unk's. You called it 'maintaining order' and could physically restrain any man using only your height and forceful personality. Your goal," you always said, "was *zero* damage."

Julia gave me a shoulder squeeze. "Got it. No worries. That dick Sheriff is probably just jealous. Somebody else touching his wife's pussy and giving her pleasure."

Chuckling, she added, "So you and Leigh cooked up your little Nancy Drew scheme and played like Lucy and Ethel to get all the evidence in case the

184

authorities said you were engaged in illegal activities?"

"That's exactly right."

"You were really taking a chance with all your little reindeer games," Julia said, shaking her head. "Thank goodness, you two didn't end up like Thelma and Louise."

"You make me laugh but, luckily, we won that round. We'll see what happens today, and thanks for being on our team."

I opened one side of the big glass doors and Julia followed me inside. Everybody else was waiting in the lobby by the desk to hear instructions.

"It's go time. When the Sheriff comes up, I'd like you all, with the exception of Leigh and Julia, to back away from the doors. It would be great if this could be handled without letting him in and just communicating through the glass. We'll see."

Jerry stepped forward, gave me a hug and whispered, "Where's your magic charm?"

I pointed to Julia.

He smiled and nodded. "Good call. None better."

I scanned the room. How wonderful it was to call everyone here a friend. Maybe this was the love the Dragonfly meant. A circle of love, given and received, was so personal, so healing, so accepting, so forgiving, and so very, well, heartwarming. Certainly better than the abusive and chaotic life I'd been living with that alcoholic Frank.

"Shhh." I put a finger to my lips.

Was that a dog barking?

I signaled to everyone to move back as Julia and Leigh stepped forward beside me. We waited. Sure enough, the Sheriff, two other officers and a large

185

dog—all in Kevlar vests—came up the circular staircase, walking in far enough to stand as close as possible to the locked glass doors. If this show of force was a deliberate attempt to put me off balance, it was working.

Wanting the clearest vision, I got near enough to the glass to make it fog up when I breathed. Julia pulled me back.

"Let him see me first. I'm bigger and taller."

"Open this door. We have a warrant to inspect the premises." The Sheriff's voice, an angry growl, was punctuated with constant barking from the dog.

"No. You have no reason to come in here," Julia's tone was cold and exact.

"Who the fuck are you?"

"She's the manager," I yelled through the doors.

Julia turned to me with a questioning look as I mouthed, "Newly hired."

"We can do this the easy way, the hard way or my way. If you don't open up," the Sheriff threatened, "we're busting down these doors and coming in."

"Just try it," I shouted from behind Julia. "It's bulletproof."

I hoped it was bulletproof.

The Sheriff waved to one of the other cops who came closer. Pressing something directly onto the door, there was a piercing sonic alarm with red flashing lights as the glass shattered into a million microscopic shards, falling down like rain.

"Oh, shit. A spring-loaded auto emergency escape tool," Jerry shouted as he ran and pulled me out of the way of flying glass.

As my reaching fingers touched the warmth of his

outstretched hands, I felt safe—from the glass. But there was no safe cover from that Sheriff.

Despite heavy breathing and a pounding heart, I tried to shrug off the electrifying shock of the over-the top-police action. My plan was a bit hazy but I had promised the fierce little Dragonfly I'd give it a try. As I stepped through crunching glass and stood in the empty doorway blocked by the Sheriff's body, I couldn't help but notice his dark eyes—cool enough to melt an arctic iceberg. Although he looked like the stereotypical fleshy, heavy-set Sheriff, those dead, dark eyes told me everything I needed to know.

His dog stood alert but motionless—head raised, ears tipped forward and eyes fixed. I could see his hackles were up; his nostrils flared and quivered but as I made deeper eye contact, his demeanor softened. Crouching down, I carefully extended my arm and offered a handful of biscuits to the dog that was the spitting image of my Gunny except for a darker face. The dog whimpered, sniffed my hand and gobbled them up.

"Shit! No!" the Sheriff yelled. "You're supposed to be a freakin' police dog!"

The poor thing looked confused. With foamy strings of spittle and crumbs falling from his muzzle, he snarled and stood at attention.

"What's his name?" I asked.

"What the fuck do you care what the dog's name is? It's Shotgun."

"Oh my God, Sheriff," I said, holding up my phone with a picture of Gunny. "Look, this is a picture of my dog Gunshot."

"Man, they do look alike. Wait a minute, are you

trying to distract me from my job?"

The Sheriff's body language and tough talk told me not to push it. I put my hands up and smiled. "I'm here in peace."

And in love.

The Sheriff squinted his eyes. "What does that mean?"

"It means let's talk this over. I think you may want to see some of our evidence."

"Evidence? You're the ones carrying on an unlawful and criminal activity."

"Well, yes, there are some murky grey areas but I need to question the legitimacy of the exact same type of massage for men taking place behind the Courtside Diner."

"Careful. Do you know why that restaurant is called the Courtside Diner? It's because the County Court resides two doors down the street. I'm in that building at least three times a week, and I know a lot of people in very high places."

"I'm sure you do. And I'm sure those people know you're running for reelection for Sheriff in November, only three months away."

"And that's why if I close you down and let everyone know what goes on here, I will be seen as a 'Savior of Sinful Activity' and win my reelection."

"Not if we show our evidence to *The Pleasant Hill Post*."

"That's bullshit. Show me what you've got."

"This is my business partner, Leigh," I said, motioning to her to step forward. "She will flip through our little cell phone show and tell."

"Here is one of the hallways," she said, "where the

men wait for their turn to get a massage and a happy ending."

"That's nothing," the Sheriff mumbled. "It's a fuckin' hallway. Next?"

"Next, here's a man being jerked off in one of the rooms by a topless masseuse."

"Crap! I think that's me." The face of the officer looking over the Sheriff's shoulder at Leigh's phone suddenly went grim.

"Now this is interesting," Leigh exclaimed, clicking through the photos, then stopping. "It seems this white limo, full of sexy Russian girls in skimpy outfits, was sent out from the Courtside Diner to the airport to pick up state dignitaries and 'entertain' them. What happened after that and what deals were made, we don't know exactly. But certainly, when questioned in court under oath, they would have to tell the truth. And for your information, videotaping is legal under the First Amendment. In New Jersey it's called the Right to Record."

"So Sheriff," I continued as I bent down and gave Shotgun a pet and scratch behind the ear, "wouldn't it be damaging to your upcoming campaign to see newspaper articles and photos, above the fold, of course, about police on shift breaks getting hand jobs? The headline might read something like: 'Protection for Services' or 'Sheriff's Office Turns a Blind Eye.'"

The Sheriff's shoulders couldn't have slumped down any further. But Leigh added insult to injury.

"Here's what we're going to do if you don't acquiesce to our demands. As we speak, we have girlfriends making up these posters," she said, giving the Sheriff time to read off her phone.

189

Sisters Unite
This is Only the Beginning
Equality for Women
All for One, One for All
The Future Is Female
We Will Not Be Silenced
Together We Move Forward
Women's Rights Are Human Rights
We Stand United
Sexual Democracy Now
We March On
Women of the World Unite
No More Faked Orgasms
Sexual Victors, Not Sexual Victims

"When they are finished we will organize! And hold these signs high and march in front of the Courtside Diner protesting injustice. It's the American way."

"Well, it's not my fault certain activities are going on at the back end of the Courtside Diner."

"No, but as the 'Savior of Sinful Activity,' you *are at fault* for not stopping it. The same way you want to stop us. And another thing, are any of the Courtside Russian girls trafficked? You know, exploited for sexual services?"

"Absolutely not. They work for themselves. I know them all. They have families, too. There's Katya, Nadia, Arina and Tanya. Feel free to talk to them anytime. So what are your demands? Money for your silence about Courtside?"

"No. We want gender equality. To be treated

exactly the way you deal with the Courtside business. In other words, not to be harassed or closed."

"That's it? You don't want me to shut down the Courtside activities?"

"No. Just replace the glass door here and leave us alone."

"And you won't alert the press?"

"No."

After a pause I put out my hand. The Sheriff shook it.

"Is this the part where you read me the *Declaration of Independence* and sing, *God Bless America*?"

"If you'd like." I noted his sarcasm and at the same time felt the warm glow of relief. "It makes for a good closer."

"Is it possible you girls could just get a manicure and call it a hand job?"

"Nope."

Bending down, I buried my nose in Shotgun's fur and looked into his eyes. He licked my face.

Chapter Twenty-Seven ⊁

MY THOUGHTS SPUN AND MY EMOTIONS skidded and whirled as I stood in the center of a sea of pulverized glass. The two policemen had gone, and so had the Sheriff and his dog. But there was something about that dog. The steady, compelling expression reflected in his eyes. I was drawn in, and my heart turned over in response.

"Suz, you were unbelievable," Jerry said as he rushed toward me. "You really took that Sheriff down. Actually, in sort of a nice way."

His smile beamed in approval as he grabbed my shoulders holding me up as much as hugging me.

"I almost lost my nerve, Jerry. But an indefinable sense of rightness swept over me, and I knew I had to stay strong. After that I felt totally immune to intimidation."

"And man, did that Sheriff buckle when we showed him those photos," Leigh exclaimed, jumping up and down while hugging her new love Steve.

"Beautifully done, Suzanne." Julia broke into an easy smile. "You were tactful and considerate. Was that your original plan?"

"No, at first I wanted to hurt him with our facts and photos. Grind it in and make him beg and crawl.

Then, by an unusual circumstance, I was moved to try a loving approach. Actually, I'm beginning to realize that making better decisions earlier means fewer regrets later. So in the end the Sheriff and I had a little bonding moment."

"Nice, but weren't you afraid of his dog?"

"The Sheriff thinks he's a trained four-legged killing machine. Turns out that dog's no man eater, just a man lover."

"And by the way, what's with giving me the manager title?"

"That was for real. I was hoping to ask if you wanted the job. I'd like to go back and finish my degree, maybe even go to law school. Please say yes. You'd be great. And no drunks to deal with!"

"It's perfect for me. I accept, and thank you. Do you happen to have anything for Isa? She has a manicurist's license."

"Hmm, interesting. She can set up and do nails right here in the other corner across from the coffeemaker. How's that? She and Javier seem to be hitting it off. Don't you think?"

"More than that!" Julia grinned, knowing it was what I needed and wanted to hear.

"Let's all go to Pam's Place for a late lunch," Leigh shouted, clapping and waving her hands. "My treat, everyone!"

"I'll meet you there, Leigh. I need to clean up this mess before clients come in tomorrow."

"I'll help you, Suz," Jerry volunteered.

"Thanks, you two," Leigh winked, "but don't stay too long so we can all enjoy our victory for women together."

"We'll hurry, Leigh. I promise." My smile echoed the warm tone in my voice. "I wouldn't miss our celebration for anything."

I thought about vacuuming the floor but the glass might clog the machine and cut into some of the hoses. Crouching down, I began the laborious task of using a brush to sweep the glass shards into a dustpan.

"You have a great ass," Jerry said, watching me intently, his gaze sliding downward.

"My greatest *ass*et, you always told me."

"Why don't we go in one of the back rooms and have a closer look?"

His words brought on that familiar clit tingle I found difficult to ignore. "Okay, but we've got to hurry. I promised we'd be there soon."

"Fast. Warp speed. Time me."

"Do I get anything out of this warp speed?"

"No talking. We're on the clock."

In one smooth move, Jerry took my hand, pulling me up from my squatting position, and led me into Room Three. "Time saver: Leave on your bra and panties, and I'll keep on my boxers."

In seconds after we partially disrobed, Jerry sat on a chair with his back to the wall. "Come, sit on my lap."

I began to lower myself down but he stopped me as he leaned back.

"No kissing? Your kisses turn me on."

"Kissing later. You're going to like this. You'll see." Jerry's stiff erection was already stabbing through his underwear. "But first, suck. Suck hard."

I took his dick in my mouth and quickly increased the suction. As I moved my lips up and down, his big swollen cock got even harder. Pumping my hand in a tight grip right below my lips and speeding up the pace, I listened for the moans. But instead, he put his hands on my shoulders.

"Now stop. Turn around, sit on my dick and take it all in your hot, wet cunt."

"Oh God, fill me up."

I was already wet and becoming soaked as Jerry took my breasts out of my bra and prodded and pinched them as I rode the pleasure-pain edge. His fingers on one hand continued pulling my nipples while the other hand cupped my pussy, opening me up with his fingers. I shuddered and electricity pulsed a direct line to my clit as I pulled my panties to the side and hovered over his waiting dick. Lowering down, little by little, my inner walls swallowed him and the fucking motion of our bodies in sync was a powerful sexual rhythm. He drove into me over and over, and I sensed he was going to climax. But I began to get the feelings of spiraling upward and flying into my own orgasm. Almost there. Almost there.

"Yes, yes, yes, keep going. Ahhh—"

Between the reverberating in my clit and his pulsating penis inside me, we both crumpled on each other sweat slicked, spent and gasping for breath.

Finally, Jerry lifted me to my feet. "Time?"

"Who knows, I was busy. And so were you. Did you enjoy it?"

"Holy shit, yes! That position is called The Wallbanger."

"Funny, I didn't hear you banging the walls."

"No, Suz. You were."

"YAY, YOU'RE HERE. We saved two seats," Leigh called out as Jerry and I hurried into Pam's Place.

Joining our eight friends and colleagues at the large middle table, everyone continued to celebrate, with high fives all around. It was the successful end of legal trouble and the possible closing of our spa.

After I clinked a spoon on my water glass several times for attention, I opened up. "I want to thank you all for your support and cooperation. At Dragonfly we now can champion the #UsToo movement for *ALL* women."

"Is that the look of complete satisfaction on your face?" Javier spoke up, smiling.

"No, that is the look of empowerment. Honest to freaking God *EMPOWERMENT!*"

Everyone burst into shouting and applause.

Soon after the excitement settled down, I excused myself, told Jerry to order me a Southwest salad and walked toward the corner by the kitchen. Sally's husband, the Sheriff, sat eagerly downing four pork chops, a separate plate piled high with mashed potatoes smothered in gravy, apple sauce and string beans. A huge slab of chocolate cake was waiting on the side. I delayed disturbing him while eating, but when he saw me, he looked up.

"Want something to eat at the grownup table?" he said, teasing but a put-down, for sure.

"I just wanted to thank you for your consideration and understanding of what we're trying to do at Dragonfly."

His smile turned down a notch. "I don't

understand a thing about it. I just don't want any crap from you girls before my reelection."

"Here's a quick refresher course," I said as I sat down in the other chair at his table for two. "Your package is on the outside, right?"

"You, uh, mean my, you know," he whispered, looking down at his lap.

"Yep. That's why it's easy for men like you to go to the Courtside. Bam! One and done. But Sally is different. For her it's an inside job."

"Sally! What the hell do you know about her, uh whatever?"

"Her pussy?"

The Sheriff started to stand.

"Sit down, Don. Let me finish. Did you know Sally loves *you* very much? She wants *you* exploring her female parts and *you* giving her mind-blowing orgasms. Can you work on that?"

"Sure, I know about the clitoris," he said, lowering his voice and sitting back down.

"The clit. That's just a start. You need to read up or, better yet, ask Sally how she likes to be touched. She'd love to give you a lesson. Wouldn't that be fun?"

"Well, yes, but she gets embarrassed," his eyes narrowing down. "You know, being a little heavier than she'd like to be."

"Uh, Don, I don't like sayin' but you've got a bit of a weight problem, too. How about you and Sally going to the gym together? I bet you could show her how to use all the equipment there. And then maybe she wouldn't have to show you her love by feeding you so much food. And you by eating it."

"Maybe. I'm going to talk to her about all this," his mood suddenly lighter. "I bet more understanding of her means more sex for me, right?"

"I think you've hit on something. But know the real answer is always *love.*"

"Yes. Thank you for that, and I'll tell you what happens."

Uh oh. I'm no sex therapist.

"Okay, Don. I'm always here to listen. But you can do this."

"By the way," he said with an odd but sort of sweet expression on his face, "you might like to take a look at Shotgun's puppies. Another police dog Bullet just had a litter two months ago. The three males, Skeet, Glock and Target, have been adopted but two females, Pistol and Ammo, are left. Come by the station and see them anytime."

"I'd love to and maybe get one. But can their names be changed? I'm not that much of a firearms girl."

"Well," he paused with an eye roll, "does it have to be Daffodil or Petunia?"

"No, but how about Sally, after your hard-working wife. And maybe I'll bring Leigh. She likes dogs, too. She could get the other one and name her Rosy for her Aunt Rose."

"Lucky dogs, Rosy and Sally. I like that. Come tomorrow and bring your girlfriend. The pups look like little versions of Shotgun."

"We'll be there. And who knows, Don? We might even vote for you in November."

BACK IN MY SEAT JERRY WANTED to know what was going on. Not much, just more bonding, I told him, not wanting to break the Sheriff's anonymity—something I learned about in Al-Anon. Jerry excused himself and hustled into the kitchen to help Sally carry out the food as Julia came over to my seat.

"Everything okay?" Only two words but uncertainty in her voice.

"Better than okay," I said, my face spreading into a smile. "One of the female police dogs recently had five puppies. Don said I could have one or two."

"Well, well. That badass Sheriff of Nottingham turned out to be a holly, jolly Santa Claus, didn't he?"

"Amazing what letting a little love into the heart will do."

AFTER ARRANGING ALL THE PLATES of Sally's food on the table, Jerry got up to welcome some new people into the restaurant. Wait! It was Mom and John. I waved to them, puzzled.

"Jerry, what's happening?"

"Okay, Sally, we're ready," he yelled toward the back as the kitchen door opened.

Sally, holding hands with her husband, Don the Sheriff, came toward me followed by Shotgun with a bouquet of flowers in his mouth.

"Sit and drop it," Jerry said, giving the dog a pet and taking the flowers.

Turning to me, Jerry got down on one knee and gave me the bouquet. "Suzanne, I'm the happiest I've ever been these last few weeks. I want us to be together always. The stars are aligned now and, if you accept, I promise you two things besides going ring shopping tomorrow. One, to tell you every day how beautiful you are. And two, to tell you every day how much I love you. Will you marry me?"

"Yes, Jerry, yes. A thousand times over."

I threw my arms around his neck and looked into his beautiful deep blue eyes filled with love. "Yes, Yes, Yes!"

The whole restaurant burst into shouts of joy and applause, along with Shotgun's nonstop barking. There was only one thing missing. I shifted in my seat, enabling me to catch a sideways glance out the window. And there it was, the distinctive, unmistakable iridescent blue-green fluttering against the glass of dragonfly wings. Silently, the words flowed from my heart.

Dragonfly, I owe it all to you.

Acknowledgments ⊁

To Peter: Best husband, best companion, best father, best lover. How lucky can one girl get?

To Mark DiIonno: Neighbor, dear friend, extraordinary columnist and novelist. His encouragement and teaching enabled me to take my writing to a higher level.

To the women and men who shared naughty conversation, personal stories and volunteered information and quotes: LD, LT, JLS, JA, RS. The rest know who you are. Hugs all around.

To Karen H. Miller, Editor/Publisher of Open Door Publications, and writers Sherri Lynn, Jack Saarela, Janice Detrie and art director Eric Labacz. Your motivation and support were there. Always.

About the Author ⌖

Logan Lansing currently lives in New Jersey, not far from New York City, and spends summers in the Adirondacks or at the Jersey shore. She loves every dog she ever met and every cat that jumps into her lap.

Although Logan has written in a variety of other genres, *Dragonfly Girl* is her first erotic romance. No matter what category, her writing always has purpose that defines, draws and guides.

When not at the computer, Logan does a high intensity-boxing workout, appreciates a deep tissue massage and enjoys a good breakfast and stimulating conversation at a local diner.

Every day is an adventure to Logan as long as it includes fun, friends, family and fantasy.